"I hate it when you touch me," Samantha choked out.

"Hate? Well, let's just try a little exercise to test the strength of this so-called hatred…."

The next thing she knew, André's mouth was against hers. Her senses went into a tailspin as the feeling of familiarity completely overwhelmed her. She knew this mouth. She knew its feel, its shape and its sensual mobility as it coaxed her own mouth to respond. She whimpered as sensation after familiar sensation went clamoring through her system.

He stepped back. She just stood there staring up at him.

"Yes…" he hissed down at her in soft-voiced triumph. "You might think you hate my touch, *cara mia*, but you cannot get enough of my kisses."

And just like that, the familiarity disappeared and she found herself looking at a complete stranger.

Amnesia

**What the memory has lost,
the body never forgets**

An electric chemistry with
a disturbingly familiar stranger...
A reawakening of passions long forgotten...
And a compulsive desire to get to know that
stranger all over again!

A compelling miniseries from
Harlequin Presents® featuring top-selling authors.

Michelle Reid

THE UNFORGETTABLE HUSBAND

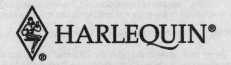

HARLEQUIN®

TORONTO • NEW YORK • LONDON
AMSTERDAM • PARIS • SYDNEY • HAMBURG
STOCKHOLM • ATHENS • TOKYO • MILAN • MADRID
PRAGUE • WARSAW • BUDAPEST • AUCKLAND

ISBN 0-373-12205-5

THE UNFORGETTABLE HUSBAND

First North American Publication 2001.

Copyright © 2001 by Michelle Reid.

Visit us at www.eHarlequin.com

Printed in U.S.A.

CHAPTER ONE

BLACK bow-tie hanging loose around his neck and the top two buttons on his snowy white dress shirt tugged open at his darkly tanned throat, André Visconte sat sprawled in the chair behind his desk, with his feet propped up on the top and the blunt-ended fingers of one beautifully shaped hand lightly clasping a squat crystal glass half full of his favourite whisky.

It was late and he was tired so his eyes were shut, the grooves around his thirty-four-year-old, life-toughened mouth seeming more harshly etched than usual. He should have gone straight home from the gala opening of a friend's new downtown restaurant but instead he had come back here to his office. He was expecting a call from Paris and it seemed more sensible to wait for it here than at his home since the office was closer.

And anyway, home held no welcome for him any more.

Some bright spark somewhere had once made the classic remark that home was where the heart was. Well, André no longer believed he had a heart, so home, these days, tended to be any place he could lay his head. And, depending on where he was, that usually meant one of the plush city residences he possessed in most capitals of the world.

Not that he had used many of them recently, if you didn't count his apartment right here in New York, of course. Though all of his homes were maintained to his expected high standards—just in case he decided to drop in.

Or in case Samantha did.

Samantha… The fingers around the whisky glass tightened fractionally. His tough mouth straightened into a line of such grim cynicism that if anyone had been there to see it happen, they would have been backing right off in alarm by now.

Because André Visconte wasn't known for his good temper these days—hadn't been known for it for twelve long months now.

Not since Samantha had walked out of his life never to be seen or heard from again. Nowadays, only a fool would dare to say her name out loud in his presence and, since fools were not suffered gladly in the Visconte empire, none ever said it.

But he couldn't stop the cursed name from creeping into his own head now and then. And when it did, it was difficult to it to unravel the gamut of different emotions that came buzzing along with it. Pain was one of them, plus a dark, bloody anger aimed entirely at himself for letting her get away from him.

Then there were the moments of real guilt-ridden anguish to contend with, or the bouts of gut-wrenching concern as to what had become of her. And, to top it all off, there was a hard-to-take sense of personal bitterness in knowing that she *could* leave him that made him wish he had never met her in the first place!

But most of all there was an ache. An ache of such muscle-clenching proportions that sometimes he had to fight not to groan at the power of it.

Why—? Because he missed her. No matter what, no matter when, no matter why—sometimes he missed her so badly that he could barely cope with what missing her did to him.

Tonight had been like that. One of those all-too-rare moments when he had caught himself laughing quite easily—actually managing to enjoy himself! Then a beautiful woman with flame-red hair had walked past him. She had reminded him of Samantha and his mood had flipped over. Light to dark. Warm to cold. Laughter to lousy misery…

After that, it had been better to escape here and brood where no one could see him doing it. But, God, he hated her for making him feel like this.

Empty. The word was empty.

The glass went to his mouth, hard lips parting so he could attack the whisky as if it was his enemy. Then, with a sigh that came from somewhere deep down inside of him, he leaned further back into the soft leather chair and waited for the whisky to attack him back by burning Samantha's name right out of his system.

It didn't happen for, being the beautiful red-haired witch that she was, she held her ground and simply paid him back for trying to get rid of her by imprinting her image on the back of his eyelids, then smiling at him provocatively.

His gut wrenched. His loins stung. His heart began to pound. 'Witch,' he breathed.

Twelve months—twelve long, miserable months—with no word from her, no sign that she was even alive. She had, in effect, simply dropped off the face of the earth as if she had never lived on it.

Cruel, heartless—*ruthless* witch.

The phone on his desk suddenly burst into life. With a reluctance that suggested he might actually be enjoying sitting here wallowing in his own misery, André let go of the glass and, without even bothering to open his eyes, reached out to hook up the receiver with a couple of long fingers, then tucked it lazily beneath his chin.

'Visconte,' he announced, voice tinged with a seductive hint of a husky drawl even though it had meant to rasp.

Expecting to hear a barrage of French come back down the line at him, he was shocked to hear the crisp clean tones of his UK-based manager assailing his ears, instead of his man in Paris.

'Nathan?' He frowned. 'What the hell—?'

Whatever Nathan Payne said to him then brought André alive as nothing else could. His eyes flicked open, revealing dark brown irises with a flash of fire. His hand snaked up to grab at the phone and his feet hit the floor with a resounding thud as he launched his lean body out of the chair.

'What—?' he raked out. 'Where—?' he barked. *'When—?'*

From the other side of the Atlantic, Nathan Payne began talking in quick, precise sentences, each one of which sent André paler until his satin gold tan had almost disappeared.

'You're sure it's her?' he asked, when his manager eventually fell into silence.

Confirmation had him sitting down again slowly—carefully, as though he needed to gauge each move he made precisely, in case he used up what was left of his suddenly depleted strength.

'No, I'm sure you couldn't,' he responded to something Nathan said to him. The hand he'd lifted up to cover his eyes was trembling slightly. 'How did it happen?'

Explanation had him raking up the whisky glass and

swallowing its contents in one tense gulp. 'And you saw this in a newspaper?' He couldn't believe it. Couldn't believe any of it.

Samantha… His dark head wrenched to one side as a very familiar pain went slicing through him.

'No!' he ground out at whatever the other man had suggested. 'Just watch her, but don't, for God's sake, do anything else!' And suddenly he was on his feet again. 'I'm on my way,' he announced. 'Just don't so much as let her out of your sight until I get there!'

The phone hit its cradle with a resounding crash. The hard sound was still echoing around the room when he thrust his body into movement. Then he was grimly striding towards the door with his face still showing the kind of reeling shock that would have rendered most people immobile…

He was there again, Samantha noticed. Sitting at the same table he had been sitting at last night, and watching her in a kind of half surreptitious way that said he didn't want her to know he was doing it.

Why, she had no idea.

She didn't recognise him. His clean-shaven fair-skinned face sounded no chords in her memory to offer a hint that she might have known him once, in a different setting or another life maybe.

Another life.

Having to smother the desire to heave out a sigh, she turned away to begin making up the order for drinks Carla had just given her. With a deftness of hand she fed two glasses under the gin optic while the other hand hooked up two small bottles of tonic and neatly knocked off the clamp tops.

'You do that like a professional,' Carla remarked
dryly, watching all of this from the other side of the bar.

Do I? Samantha mused as she placed the items down
on Carla's tray. Well, there's something else that could
belong to that other life I can't remember. 'Do you want
draught beer or the bottled stuff?'

'The bottled—are you feeling all right?' Carla asked,
frowning, because it wasn't like Samantha not to rise to
a bit of pleasant banter when she was given the chance
to.

'Just tired,' she said, and limped off down the bar to
get the two bottled beers from the chiller, reassured that
her answer had some justification since neither she nor
Carla should be working in the hotel lounge bar tonight.
Officially, their job was looking after Reception. But the
hotel was teetering on its very last legs. Business was
poor, and the hotel was being run with the minimum of
staff, which therefore meant that people had to chip in
wherever they happened to be needed.

Like this week, for instance, when the two of them
were doubling up shifts by running the bar in the evening and the reception during the day.

But that didn't mean she was feeling so tired that she
was imagining a pair of eyes burning into her every time
she turned her back. Limping back down the bar with
the two requested beers, she took a glance sideways and
just caught the stranger's eyes on her before he looked
away.

'The man sitting on his own,' she murmured to Carla.
'Any idea who he is?'

'You mean the well-scrubbed, good-looking one in
the Savile Row suit?' she quizzed, adding at Samantha's
nod, 'Nathan Payne. Room two-one-two, if his charge
slips are to be believed. He booked in last night when

Freddie was on duty. And here on business—which doesn't surprise me, because I can't believe a man like him would actually *choose* this place for a holiday.'

Her derision was clear, and Samantha didn't dispute it. Though the Tremount Hotel's setting was outstandingly good, sitting right on the edge of its own headland in a beautiful part of Devon, it had been let go so badly that Carla hadn't been joking when she'd suggested the stranger would not choose it for a holiday. Few people did.

'Rumour has it that he works for one of the huge hotel conglomerates,' Carla went on. 'The ones which buy up run-down monstrosities like this place and turn them into super-modern, ultra-select holiday complexes like the ones you see further down the coast.'

Was that what he was doing—just checking out the whole hotel in general, and not just watching her? Relief quivered through her. Her face relaxed. 'Well, not before time, I suppose,' she opined, feeling much better now she had a solid reason for the man's presence here. 'The old place could certainly do with a major face-lift.'

'But at the expense of all our jobs?' Carla quizzed. 'The hotel will have to close to renovate, and where will that leave us?'

On that decidedly now sombre note, she picked up her tray and walked away, leaving Samantha alone with her words to chew upon. For what was she going to do if the hotel closed? The Tremount might be suffering from age and neglect, but it had thrown her a lifeline when she'd desperately needed one. She didn't just work here, she also *lived* here. The Tremount was her home.

The stranger left quite early. Around nine o'clock he glanced at his watch, stood up and threw some money down on the table for Carla, then moved quickly out of the room. There was something very purposeful in the way he did it. As though he was going somewhere special and was running late.

A suspicion Freddie confirmed when he strolled into the lounge a few minutes later. 'That guy from the Visconte Group left in a hurry,' he remarked. 'He strode out the hotel, gunned up his Porsche, then shot off up the driveway like a bat out of hell.'

'Maybe he couldn't stand the thought of spending another night sharing a bathroom with eight other guest rooms,' Carla suggested. 'No *ensuites* at the Tremount,' she mocked. 'Here, you learn to tough it out or run!'

'If he was running, he went without paying his bill,' Freddie said. 'More like he was meeting someone,' he decided. 'The London train was due in Exeter around— Sam?' he cut in suddenly. 'Are you feeling all right? You've gone a bit pale.'

Had she? Funnily enough she felt quite pale—which was a very strange sensation in itself. It was the name, *Visconte*. For a brief moment there, she'd thought she knew it.

Which was a novelty in itself, because names never usually meant anything to her.

Names, faces, places, dates...

'I'm fine,' she said, and tossed out a smile for the benefit of the other two. 'Are you here for your usual, Freddie?' she asked, lightly passing off the moment.

But the name remained with her for the rest of the evening. And every so often she would think, *Visconte*, and find herself going off into a strange blank trance. A memory? she wondered. A brief flash from her past that had disappeared as quickly as it had come?

If it was, she couldn't afford to let it go by without checking it out, she decided. And, since the Visconte name was linked with the stranger, she resolved to ask him about it at the first opportunity, because what other hope did she have of ever knowing who she was, unless she attempted to do it herself? With twelve long months behind her of waiting for someone else to do it for her, she had to start accepting that it just wasn't going to happen.

Only last week the local paper had run yet another full-page spread on her plight, then pleaded for anyone who might recognise her to come forward. No one had. The police had finally come to the conclusion that she must have been alone in the world and on holiday here in Devon when the accident had happened. The car she had been driving was completely burned out—to the extent that they could only tell it had once been a red Alfa Romeo. They'd had no reports of a missing red Alfa Romeo. No reports of a woman gone missing *driving* a red Alfa Romeo.

Sometimes it felt as if she had died out there on that lonely road the night the petrol tanker had hit her, only to come back to life again many weeks later as a completely different human being.

But she wasn't a different human being, she told herself firmly. She was simply a lost one who needed to find herself. If she hung onto nothing else then she had to hang on tight to that belief.

Eleven o'clock saw the lounge bar empty. Samantha rubbed her aching knee and finished tidying behind the bar. An hour later she was safely tucked up in bed, and by eight-thirty the next morning, after a restless night dreaming about dark demons and roaring dragons, both she and Carla were back on duty behind Reception, doing the job they were officially paid to do.

It was changeover day so the foyer was busy, but

Samantha kept an eye out for Mr Payne, determined to speak to him if she was given the opportunity.

That opportunity arrived around lunch-time. The reception area had just cleared for the first time that morning, and only a few stragglers now hung around the foyer waiting for taxis to take them to the station. She and Carla were busy working out room allocations for the new guests that would be arriving throughout the afternoon when Samantha happened to glance up as the old-fashioned entrance doors begin to rotate and none other than Mr Payne strode in.

He paused just inside the foyer, and Samantha made the quick decision to take her chance while she had it. Murmuring, 'Excuse me for a minute,' to Carla, she opened the lift-top section in their workstation and stepped quickly through it—only to go still when she saw another man walk in and pause at Mr Payne's side.

Both men were tall, both lean, both dressed in the kind of needle-sharp suits you wouldn't find anywhere but at a top-notch tailors. But the newcomer was taller and a lot darker, and just that bit more...forbidding because of it, she observed with a cold little quiver that stopped her from approaching them.

As she watched, she saw his dark brown eyes make an impatient scan of their surroundings. There was a tension about him, a restlessness so severely contained that it flicked along his chiselled jawline as if he was clenching and unclenching his teeth behind his rather cold-looking mouth. Then the mouth suddenly twisted, and Samantha didn't need to be clairvoyant to know what he was thinking right then.

The decor in here was a horrendous mix of pre-First World War splendour and 1960s grot. Originally built to grand Victorian specifications, the Tremount had been revamped in the 1960s, and everything tasteful had been pulled out or hidden behind sheets of flat plasterboard. Even the carpet on the floor was a gruesome spread of royal purple with large splashes of sunshine-gold to complete the horror. There wasn't a stick of furniture in the place that said grace and style; instead it said teak and vinyl rubbish, and even the rubbish had seen better days.

Much like herself, she likened wryly, absently rubbing her knee while watching his gaze go slashing right past her. Then it stopped, sharpened, and came swinging swiftly back again.

Their eyes locked. The hard line of his mouth slackened on a short, sharp intake of air. He looked horrified. And suddenly she didn't like what was happening here. She didn't like *him*, she realised, as a tight constriction completely closed her throat. She couldn't breathe, couldn't swallow. Even her heart stopped beating with a violent thump, then set going like a hammer drill against her right temple.

As if he could see it happen, his eyes flicked up to her temple. She saw him flinch—remembered the fine pink pucker of scar tissue there, and instinctively put up a hand to cover it.

The fact that she'd managed to move seemed to prompt him to do the same. He began walking straight towards her in a strange, slow, measured way that made her want to start backing. Sweat began to break out all over her. The room began to fade, tunnelling inwards in ever-decreasing circles until the only the two people left in the foyer seemed to be herself and him. And the closer he came, the more tight and airless the tunnel began to feel, until she was almost suffocating by the time he came to a halt two short feet away.

And he was big—too big. Too dark, too handsome, too—everything, she finished on a fine, tight shudder. Overpowering her with his presence, with that compelling look burning in his eyes.

No, she protested, though she had no idea what it was she was protesting against.

Maybe she'd said the word out loud, because he suddenly went quite pale, and his eyes were so dark she actually felt as if she was being drawn right into them.

Crazy, she told herself. Don't be crazy.

'Samantha,' he breathed very thickly. 'Oh, dear God…'

She fainted. With her name still sounding in her head, she simply closed her eyes and sank like a stone to the purple and gold carpet.

CHAPTER TWO

IN ALL of the long days and weeks she had spent in pain in hospital, she hadn't fainted. In all of the long, dreadfully frightening weeks and months which had accompanied her slow recovery, she had never fainted. Of all the things she had ever wished and hoped and prayed for during the last twelve empty months, it had been for someone to come in through those revolving doors and say her name to her.

Yet, when someone had done exactly that, she'd fainted.

Samantha came round thinking all of that, in a mad and bewildering jumble of confusion, to find herself lying on one of the reception sofas with Carla squatting beside her, urgently chafing one of her hands, and the sounds of other people talking in hushed voices just beyond her vision.

'Are you all right?' Carla said anxiously the moment she saw Samantha open her eyes.

'He knows me,' she whispered. 'He knows who I am.'

'I know,' Carla murmured gently.

The stranger suddenly appeared over Carla's shoulder. Still too big, still too dark, too—

'I'm sorry,' he rasped out. 'Seeing you was such a shock that I just didn't think before I acted.' He stopped, swallowed tensely, then added. 'Are you okay, *cara*?'

She didn't answer. Her mind was too busy trying to grapple with the frightening fact that this man actually seemed to know her, while she looked at him and saw

17

a total stranger! It wasn't fair—it wasn't! The doctors had suggested that a shock like this might be all that was needed to bring her memory back.

But it hadn't. Sheer disappointment had her eyes fluttering shut again.

'No.' His thick voice pleaded roughly. 'Samantha—don't pass out again. I'm not here to—'

His hand touched her shoulder. Her senses went haywire, crawling through her body like scattering spiders and flinging her into a whirling mad panic that jolted her into a sitting position to violently thrust his hand away.

'Don't touch me…' she gasped out in shuddering reaction. 'I don't know you. *I don't!*'

There was a muttered expletive, then Mr Payne appeared. His fair-skinned face was lined with concern as he murmured something soothing in Italian to the other man. He answered in the same language then, quite suddenly, spun on his heel and sat down abruptly on a nearby chair, as if the strength had just been wrenched out of him. And only then did it occur to Samantha that if he did really know her then he too must be suffering from shock.

'Here…' Carla pushed a glass of water at her. 'Drink some of this,' she urged. 'You look dreadful.'

The stranger's head came up, shock-darkened eyes honing directly onto her own, and for a moment Samantha felt herself sinking into those blackened depths again, as if drawn there by something more powerful than logic.

Oh, God. Confused, she wrenched her gaze away, pushing the glass aside so she could cover her face with a hand while she at least attempted to get a hold of herself.

'Is she all right?'

'What's the matter with her?'

'Has that man upset her?'

Hearing the jumble of questions coming from all directions reminded her that there were other people present. 'Get me away from this,' she whispered to Carla.

'Of course,' Carla murmured understandingly, and straightened up before taking hold of Samantha's arm to help her to stand. It was a well-timed offer of help, because the moment she tried to put any weight on her right leg the knee reacted with a crack of pain that made her gasp out loud.

'I wondered when I saw you fall if that would happen.' Carla frowned. 'You hit your bad knee against the corner of the desk as you fainted,' she explained, looking down at the place where Samantha's uniform-straight navy blue skirt finished, just above the injury. 'I hope you've not done it any further damage.'

Gritting her teeth and clinging to Carla, she began to limp across the reception area towards a door marked 'Staff Only'.

The stranger came towering to his feet. 'Where are you going?' he said sharply, staring at her as though he was expecting her to make a sudden run for it.

Samantha smiled wanly at the prospect. She couldn't run if she tried. 'Staffroom,' she said, then added very reluctantly, 'You can come if you want.'

'I have every intention of doing so,' he replied, and moved to follow them—only to pause and turn to make a flashing inventory of the crowded foyer. 'Are you the only two people running this place?' he questioned.

American. His accent contained the deep velvet drawl of a cultured American, Samantha noticed, then began frowning in confusion, because he and Nathan Payne had been speaking in Italian to each other only a minute ago.

'The manager is away on business today.' Carla did the explaining. 'I'll just help Samantha in here, then I'll come back and—'

'No!' Samantha protested, her hand closing convulsively over Carla's. 'Don't leave me alone with him!' she whispered shrilly, not caring if the stranger had heard what she'd said and was offended by it.

'Okay,' Carla said soothingly, but her expression was looking a little hunted. It was the busiest time of the week on Reception and both of them couldn't just walk off duty.

'Nathan.' Even Samantha, in her state of shock, heard the voice of authority when it spoke like that. 'Take over here,' the stranger instructed—then, at Carla's uncertain look, 'Don't worry. He knows what he's doing. It's his job to know. We are going in here, I presume?' he then prompted smoothly, indicating the door next to the reception desk.

Samantha nodded, having to bite down on her bottom lip now because her knee was hurting so badly. So, leaning more heavily on Carla while trying hard not to show it, she limped slowly through the staffroom door with him following so close behind her that she could actually feel his breath on her neck.

She shuddered, wishing he would just back off a little and give her time to recover and think. She didn't want him here. She didn't like him. She didn't *want* to like him. Which was just stupid when she remembered that this man would be the link to her past she had been praying for.

It was relief to sit down in one of the chairs. At Samantha's mumbled request Carla hurried off to collect her painkillers from her room, and the stranger pulled up another chair right beside her own, then sank down heavily on it. It brought him too close. She could feel his body heat and smell his subtle, masculine scent. Fighting hard not to edge right away from him, she leaned forward slightly to rub at her throbbing knee.

'How bad is it?' he rasped.

'Not too bad,' she lied. In fact it was very painful. 'I just need to rest it for a few minutes.'

'I meant, how badly did you injure your knee in the accident?' he grimly corrected her mistake.

'You know about that?' she responded in surprise.

'How the hell else do you think I found you?' he bit out angrily.

She flinched at his tone; he let out a sigh and suddenly sat forward to lean his elbows on his spread knees, bringing their heads disturbingly close.

'Sorry.' He sighed. 'I didn't mean to bite your head off.'

Samantha didn't say anything, and after a moment he said more levelly, 'Nathan was surveying a couple of properties around here. He saw the article about you in the local newspaper and recognised your photograph. He couldn't believe it!' he ground out. 'Neither could I when he rang me in New York to—' The words dried up, seeming to block in his throat so he had to swallow, and his hands clenched very tightly together between his spread thighs.

'Who is Nathan?' she asked huskily.

His head swivelled round to look at her, dark brown eyes lancing her a bitter hard look. 'Don't you think it's time you asked me who *I* am?' he suggested.

But oddly, even to herself, Samantha shook her head.

She didn't know why, but she just wasn't ready to hear who he was yet.

'This man…Nathan,' she persisted instead. 'He's been staying here over the last few days to keep an eye on me, hasn't he?'

He took her refusal to take him up on his challenge with a tensing of his jaw. He answered her question though. 'Yes. After he rang me and told me about your accident and the—the—God—' He choked, had to stop to swallow thickly, lifting a decidedly shaky hand to press at his mouth. 'I don't want to think about that,' he muttered after a moment. 'I can't cope with thinking about that right now…'

'I'm sorry,' she murmured, accepting that if he had read the article the newspaper had run on her accident, then he had a right to feel this bad about it. It made horrendous reading.

But she didn't accept the cruel way he lashed back at her. 'For surviving when six other people didn't?'

The harsh words sent her jerking back in her seat in reaction, her green eyes spitting ice as a cold anger suddenly took her over. 'I feel no sense of pleasure in being the lucky one,' she informed him frigidly. 'Six people died. I survived. But if you think I've spent the last year counting my blessings at their expense then you couldn't be more wrong!'

'And I've spent the last year wishing you in hell,' he sliced back at her. 'Only to discover that you were already living there and I didn't know a damned thing about it!'

True, so true, she grimly acknowledged, for living hell was exactly where she had been. But it made her wonder why he had wished her in hell. What had she done to him to make him wish something as cruel as that upon her?

Whatever the reason, his harsh words hurt, and did nothing to make her feel more comfortable with him. In fact she was scared.

Maybe he realised it, because he launched himself back to his feet, then just stood there literally pulsing with a sizzling tension. He was tall—over six feet—and the room suddenly grew smaller. He seemed to dwarf everything—and not just with his physical presence. The man possessed a raw kind of energy that seemed to be sucking up all the oxygen.

Then he let out a harsh sigh and muttered something that sounded like a curse beneath his breath. As he did so, some of the tension eased out of the atmosphere.

'I'm not managing this very well,' he admitted finally.

No, he wasn't, Samantha agreed. But then, neither was she.

It was perhaps a good point for Carla to reappear. Glancing warily from one tense face to the other, she came to squat down in front of Samantha, then silently handed her the foil slide containing her prescription painkillers, followed by a second glass of water.

'Thanks,' she murmured, and flipped two of the tablets out into her palm, swallowed them down with the help of the water then, on a sigh, sat back in the chair and closed her eyes to wait for the tablets to take effect. The knee was throbbing quite badly, and hot to the touch, which told her she must have knocked it pretty hard.

But that was not the real reason why she was sitting with her eyes closed like this, she had to admit. It was really a means of escape from what was beginning to develop here—not that closing her eyes was going to make it all go away again, she acknowledged heavily.

He was here, and she was too acutely aware of him standing across the room like a dark shadow threatening to completely envelop her.

And on top of that it was just too quiet. Quiet enough for her to sense that he and Carla were swapping silent messages, which had to involve her, though she didn't bother to open her eyes to see exactly what it was they were plotting.

As it was, she soon found out.

'Sam…' Carla's voice sounded anxious to say the least '…do you think you will be all right now? Only I really must go and see if everything is okay out there…'

A clammy sense of dismay went trickling through her when she realised they had been silently plotting her isolation. She didn't want to be left alone with him. But she also saw that there was no sense in putting off the inevitable. And besides, she understood Carla's predicament. They were paid to do a job here, and this hotel had a poor enough reputation without the staff walking off duty.

So she gave a short nod of understanding, then forced herself to open her eyes and smile. 'Thanks. I'll be fine now.'

With another concerned scan of her pale face, then an even more concerned one of the man who was standing on the other side of the room, Carla stood up and, with a final glance at their two pale faces, left the two of them to it.

And the new silence was cloying.

Samantha didn't move a single muscle and neither did he. His attention was fixed on the view outside the staff-room window which, since it looked directly onto the hotel kitchens, was not a pretty sight. *She* kept her eyes fixed on the empty water glass she was so very carefully turning in her hands.

'What now?' she asked when she could stand the tension no longer.

'It's truth time, I suppose,' he said, sounding as reluctant about it as she felt.

Turning slowly to face her, he stood watching her for a few more tense seconds. Then he seemed to come to some kind of decision and strode over to sit himself down again—and gently reached for the glass.

His fingers brushed lightly across hers and a fine frisson set her pulse racing. Sliding the glass away, he further disturbed her by taking hold of one of her hands as he set the glass aside then turned back to her.

'Look at me,' he urged.

Her eyes lowered and fixed fiercely on their clasped hands; the command locked her teeth together. And for the life of her she couldn't move a muscle. The frisson became a deep inner tremor that vibrated so strongly she knew he could feel it.

'I know I've come as a shock, but you have to start facing this, Samantha…' he told her quietly.

He was right, and she did. But she still didn't want to.

'So begin by at least looking at me while we talk…'

Oh, dear God, she thought and tried to swallow. It took every bit of courage she had in her to lift her eyes and look directly at him.

He's so beautiful, was the first unbidden thought to filter through her like a lonely sigh. His neatly styled hair was straight and black; his skin was warmed by a tan that she'd seemed to know from the moment she'd set eyes on him was natural to him. Sleek black eyebrows, long black eyelashes, eyes the colour of dark bitter chocolate. A regular-shaped nose, she saw as her gaze drifted downward to pause at his firm but inherently sensual mouth. It was a strong face, a deeply attractive well-balanced face.

But it was still the face of a total stranger, she concluded.

A stranger who was about to insist he was no stranger and, indeed, she added frowningly to that, already he did not *feel* like a stranger, because his touch felt familiar. There was an intimacy in the way he was looking at her that told her that this man knew her only too well. Probably knew her better than she knew herself.

'Samantha,' he prompted. 'You know your name is Samantha.'

Glad of the excuse to claim her hand back, she lifted her fingers to part the collar of her blouse, revealing the necklace she wore around her throat.

A necklace spelling out her name in gold lettering. Sweet but childish though it was. 'It's all I had left,' she explained. 'Everything else was lost in the fire.'

The eyes flashed again. 'Were you burned?' he asked harshly.

Her body became shrouded in a clammy coat of perspiration. 'No.' She shook her head. 'Someone dragged me out before the car blew.' Then the trembling fingers left the necklace to quiver up to the small pink scar at her temple. 'I injured my head,' she said huskily, 'my arm...' she gave her right arm a tense little jerk '...and m-my right leg...'

His eyes dropped to her knee, where even the sensible, high-denier thickness of her stockings could not hide the scarring beneath. Then with a slow raising of his oh-too-sensual long black lashes, he looked at the scar at her temple. 'Your lovely face…' he breathed, lifting a hand up to touch the scar.

She flinched back in rejection. And for the first time in months of just being too glad to be alive to want to feel any kind of revulsion for the physically obvious damage she had survived with, Samantha experienced a terrible, terrible urge to hide herself away.

This man's fault! She blamed him wretchedly. He was so obviously one of those very rare people who was blessed with physical perfection himself and no doubt surrounded himself with the same that she suddenly knew, knew that whoever he was and whatever he once had been to her, she no longer fitted into his selective criteria!

It was her turn to get up, move away, though she didn't do it with the same grace he did! 'Who are you?' She turned to launch at him wretchedly.

He stood up. 'My name is *Visconte*,' he told her huskily. '*André* Visconte.'

There it was, 'Visconte.' She breathed the name softly. 'Of the Visconte Hotel Group?'

He nodded slowly, watching her intently for a sign that the name might begin to mean something else to her. But other than the same odd sensation she'd experienced the night before, when Freddie had said the name, it still meant nothing.

'And me?' She then forced herself to whisper. 'Who am I?'

His eyes went black again, nerve ends began to sing. 'Your name is also Visconte,' he informed her carefully, then extended very gently, 'You are my wife…'

CHAPTER THREE

FACE white, body stiff, eyes pressed tightly shut, Samantha simply stood there waiting—waiting to discover if this latest shock, coming hard upon all the other shocks she had suffered today, would manage to crash through the thick wall closing off her memory.

I am Samantha Visconte, she silently chanted. His wife. This man's wife. A man I must have loved enough to marry. A man who must have loved me enough to do the same. It should mean something. She stood there *willing* it to mean something!

But it didn't. 'No,' she said on a release of pent-up air, and opened her eyes to look at him with the same perfectly blank expression. 'The name means nothing to me.'

She might as well have slapped him. He looked away, then sat down, his lean body hunching over again as he dipped his dark head and pressed his elbows into his spread knees—but not before Samantha had seen the flash of pain in his eyes and realised that her ill-chosen words had managed to hurt him. 'I'm sorry,' she murmured uncomfortably. 'I didn't mean it to come out sounding so…'

'Flat?' he incised when she hesitated.

She ran her dry tongue around her even drier lips. 'Y-you don't understand.' She pushed out an unsteady explanation. 'The doctors have been suggesting to me for months that a shock meeting like this might be all that was needed to jolt me into…'

'I need a drink,' he cut in, then stood up and began striding quickly for the door.

Samantha watched him go—relieved he was going because she needed time alone to try to come to terms with all of this. But it didn't stop her gaze from following him, eyes feeding on his tall, lean framework as if she still couldn't quite believe that he was real.

Maybe he wasn't, she then told herself with a rueful little smile that mocked the turmoil her mind was in. Maybe this was going to turn out to be just another nightmare in a long line of nightmares where tall dark strangers visited her and claimed to know who she was.

'Have we been married long?'

Why she stopped him at the door when she'd been glad he was going, she didn't know. But the question blurted out anyway, bringing him to a halt with his hand on the door handle, and stopping her breath as she waited for him to turn.

'Two years,' he replied and there was a strangeness about his voice that bothered her slightly. 'It will be our second wedding anniversary in two days' time,' he tagged on—then left the room.

Staring at the closed door through which he had disappeared, Samantha found herself incapable of feeling anything at all now, as a different kind of numbness overcame her.

Two days, she was thinking. Which made it the twelfth. They hadn't even celebrated their first wedding anniversary together.

Her accident had occurred on the twelfth. Where had she been going on her first wedding anniversary? Had she been rushing back to be with him when the accident had happened? Had that been why she'd—?

No. She mustn't allow herself to think like that. The

police had assured her it had not been her fault. A petrol tanker had jackknifed on the wet road and ploughed into three other cars besides her own before it had burst into a ball of fire. She had been lucky because the tanker had hit her car first then left it behind, a twisted wreck as it careered on. The people in the cars behind her hadn't stood a chance because they'd caught the brunt of the explosion when everything had gone up. Other drivers had had time to pull Samantha free before her car had joined in the inferno. But her body had had to pay the price for the urgency with which they had got her out. Her head, already split and bleeding from the impact, had luckily rendered her unconscious, but they had told her the man who had pulled her free had had no choice but to wrench her crushed knee through splintered metal if he was to get her clear in time. And her arm, already fractured in three places, had been made worse because it had been the only limb the man had been able to use to tug her out.

The arm had healed now, thankfully. And the knee was getting stronger every day with the help of a lot of physiotherapy. But the scar on her face was a reminder she saw every time she looked into a mirror.

And why was she hashing over all of this right now, when she had far more important things to think about? It was crazy!

So what's new? She mocked herself, then with a sigh sat back down again.

She hadn't even considered yet whether André Visconte was lying or not, she realised. Though why someone like him would want to claim someone in her physical and psychological state unless he felt duty-bound to answer the question for her.

Because no one in their right mind would.

No one *had* for twelve long months. So why hadn't he found her before now?

He said he'd wished her in hell, she remembered. Did that mean that their marriage had already been over before their first wedding anniversary? Was that why he hadn't bothered to look for her? And had he only done so now because someone had recognised her in that newspaper as the woman who was his wife?

Agitation began to rise. Her head began to throb, bringing her fingers up to rub at her temple. I want to remember. *Please* let me remember! she pleaded silently. He'd said something about being in New York. Was that where he lived? Was that where they'd met? Yet her accent was so obviously English that even she— who had learned to question everything about herself over the last twelve, empty months—had not once questioned her nationality.

Had they met here in England? Did they have a home in this area? Was he wealthy enough to own homes in two places? Of course he was wealthy enough, she told herself crossly. He owned a string of prestigious hotels. He *looked* wealthy. His clothes positively shrieked of wealth.

So what did that make her? A wealthy woman in her own right for her to have moved in the same social circles as he?

She didn't feel wealthy. She felt poor—impoverished, in fact.

Impoverished from the inside, never mind the outer evidence, with her sensible flat-heeled black leather shoes that had been bought for comfort and practicality rather than because she could really afford them. For months her clothes had been charitable handouts, ill-fitting, drab-looking garments other people no longer wanted to wear but which had been good enough for an impoverished woman who had lost everything including her mind! It had only been since she'd landed this job here that she had been able to afford to replace them with something more respectable—cheap, chain store stuff, but at least they were new and belonged to her—only to her.

What did Visconte see when he looked at this woman he claimed was his wife?

Getting up, she went to stand by the tarnished old mirror that hung on the staffroom wall. If she ignored the scar at her temple, the reflection told her that she was quite passably attractive. The combination of long red wavy hair teamed with creamy white skin must have once looked quite startling—especially before too many long months of constant strain had hollowed out her cheeks and put dark bruises under her eyes. But some inner sense that hadn't quite been blanked off with the rest of her memory told her she had always been slender, and the physiotherapists had been impressed with what they'd called her 'athletic muscle structure'.

'Could have been a dancer,' one of them had said in a wry, teasing way meant to offset the agony he'd been putting her through as he'd manipulated her injured knee. 'Your muscles are strong, but supple with it.'

Supple, slender dancer worthy of a second look once upon a time. Not any more, though, she accepted. She thought of the stranger and how physically perfect he was, and wanted to sit down and cry.

I don't want this, she thought on a sudden surge of panic. I don't want any of it!

He can't want me. How can he want me? If I am his wife why has it taken him twelve months to find me? If he'd loved me wouldn't a man like him have been scouring the whole countryside looking for me?

I would have done for him, she acknowledged with an odd pain that said her feelings for him were not entirely indifferent, no matter what her brain was refusing to uncover.

'Oh, God.' She dropped back into the chair to bury her face in her hands as the throbbing in her head became unbearable.

Pull yourself together! she tried to tell herself. You have to pull yourself together and start thinking about what happens next, before—

The door came open. He stepped inside and closed it again, his eyes narrowing on the way she quickly lifted her face from her hands.

His jacket had gone; that was the first totally incomprehensible thing her eyes focused on. The dark silk tie with the slender knot had been tugged down a little and the top button of his shirt was undone, as if he'd found the constriction of his clothes annoying and needed to feel fresh air around that taut tanned throat.

Her mind did a dizzy whirl on a hot, slick spurt of sudden sensual awareness. 'Here…' He was walking towards her with a glass of something golden in his hand. 'I think you need one of these as much as I do.'

'No.' She shook her head. 'I can't, not on top of the painkillers—thank you all the same.'

If nothing else, the remark stopped him, mere inches away from touching her. She didn't want him to touch her—why, again she didn't know. Except—

Stranger. The word kept on playing itself over and over like some dreadful, dreadful warning. This man who said he was her husband was a total stranger to her. And the worst of it was she kept on getting this weird idea that him being a stranger to her was not a new feeling.

He discarded the glass, then stood in front of her with his hands thrust into his trouser pockets. He seemed to be waiting for something, but Samantha didn't know what, so she looked at the garish carpet between their feet and waited for whatever was supposed to come next.

What could come next? she then thought tensely. There were questions to ask. Things to know. This was the beginning of her problems, not the end of them.

'How's the knee?'

'What—?' She blinked up at him, then away again. 'Oh.' A hand automatically went down to touch the knee. 'Better now, thank you.'

Silence. Her nerves began to fray. Teeth gritted together behind clenched lips. God, she wished he would just do something! Say something cruel and trite like, Well, nice to have seen you again, sorry you don't remember me, but I have to go now!

She wished he would pull her up into his big arms and hold her, hold her tightly, until all these terrible feelings of confusion and fear went away!

He released a sigh. It sounded raw. She glanced at him warily. He bit out harshly, 'This place is the pits!'

He was right and it was. Small and shabby and way, way beneath his dignity. 'I l-love this place.' She heard herself whisper. 'It gave me a home and a life when I no longer had either.'

Her words sent his face white again—maybe he thought she was taking a shot at him. He threw himself back into the chair beside her—close to her again, his shoulder only a hair's breadth away from rubbing against her shoulder again.

Move away from me, she wanted to say.

'Listen,' he said. And she could feel him fighting something, fighting it so fiercely that his tension straightened her spine and held it so stiff it tingled like a live wire. 'We need to get away from here,' he gritted. 'Find more—private surroundings where we can—relax—'

Even he made the word sound dubious. For who could relax in a situation like this? She certainly couldn't.

'Talk,' he went on. 'Have time for you to ask the kind of questions I know you must be burning to ask, and for me to do the same.'

He looked at her for a reaction. Samantha stared straight ahead.

'We can do that better at my own hotel in Exeter than we can here,' he suggested.

'Your hotel,' she repeated, remembering the big, new hotel that had opened its doors only last year.

'Will you come?'

'I…' She wasn't at all sure about that. She wasn't sure she wanted to go anywhere with him, or leave what had become over the last year the only place where she felt safe and secure in her bewildered little world.

'It's either you come with me or I move in here,' he declared, and so flatly that she didn't for one moment think he was bluffing. 'I would prefer it to be the other way round simply because my place is about a hundred times more comfortable than this. But—' The pause brought her eyes up to look warily into his. It was what he had been aiming for. The chocolate-brown turned to cold black marble slabs of grim determination. 'I am not letting you out of my sight again—ever—do you understand that?'

Understand? She almost choked on it. 'I want proof,' she whispered.

'Proof of what?' He frowned.

'That you are who you say you are and I am who you say I am before I'll make any decisions about anything.'

She expected him to be affronted but oddly he wasn't—which in itself was proof enough that he was indeed telling her the truth about them.

Without a word he stood up, left the room again, coming back mere seconds later carrying the jacket to his suit. His hand was already fishing in the inside pocket when he came to stand over her.

'My passport,' he said, dropping the thick, bulky document onto her lap. 'Your passport—an old one, I admit, but it can still give you your *proof*.' That too landed on her knee. 'Our marriage certificate.' It landed on top of the two passports. 'And...' this came less arrogantly '...a photo...' it fluttered down onto her lap, landing face down. 'Of you and me on our wedding day.'

He'd come prepared for this, she realised, staring down at the small heap of items now sitting on her lap without attempting to touch them.

Because she was afraid to.

But why was she afraid? He had already told her who he was and who she was and what they were to each other. She was even already convinced that every word he'd said was the truth, or why else would he be standing here in this scruffy back room of a scruffy hotel in a scruffy corner of Devon saying all of these things?

So why, *why* was she feeling so afraid to actually look at the physical proof of all of that?

The answer came at her hard and cold, and frightened her more than everything else put together. She didn't want to look for the same reason she'd lost her memory in the first place. The doctors had told her it had had little to do with the car crash. The accident might have helped to cause the amnesia, but the real reason for it lay deeply rooted in some other trauma she'd found she could not face on top of all the pain she had been suffering at that time. So her mind had done the kindest thing and had locked up the personal trauma so all she had to do was to deal with the physical trauma.

Looking at these documents was going to be like squeezing open the door on that trauma, whatever it was.

'You never were a coward, Samantha,' he told her quietly, at the same time letting her know that he knew exactly what was going on inside her head.

Well, I am now,' she whispered, and her body began to tremble.

Instantly he was dropping down into the chair again, his hands coming out, covering hers where they lay pleated tightly together on her stomach, safely away from his proof. And this time she did not flinch away from his touch. This time she actually needed it.

'Then we'll do it together,' he decided gently.

With one hand still covering her two hands, he used the other to slide his passport out from the bottom of the pile and flicked it open at the small photograph that showed his beautiful features set in a sternly arrogant pose.

'Visconte', it said. 'André Fabrizio'. 'American citizen'.

'I look like a gangster,' he said, trying to lighten the moment. Closing the book, he then selected the other one.

You weren't supposed to smile on passport photographs. But the face looking back up her from her own lap told her that this person did not know how to turn that provocative little smile off. And her face wore no evidence of strain. She simply looked lively and lovely and—

'Visconte', it said. 'Samantha Jane'. 'British citizen'.

'You lost this particular passport about six months after we were married and had to apply for a new one,' he explained. 'But I happened to turn this up when I was—' He stopped, then went on. 'When I was searching through some old papers.' He finally concluded. But they both knew he had been about to say something else.

When his hand moved to pick up the marriage certificate, she stopped him. 'No.' She breathed out thickly. 'Not that. Th-the other...'

Slowly, reluctantly almost, his fingers moved to pick up the photograph, hesitated a moment, then flipped it over.

Samantha's heart flipped over with it. Because staring back at her in full Technicolor was herself, dressed up in frothy bridal-white.

Laughing. She was laughing up into the face of her handsome groom. Laughing up at *him*—this man dressed in a dark suit with a white rose in his lapel and confetti lying on his broad shoulders. He was laughing too, but there was more—so much more to his laughter than just mere amusement. There was—

Abruptly she closed her eyes, shutting it out, shutting everything out as her body began to shake violently, a clammy sweat breaking out across her chilled flesh. She couldn't breathe again, couldn't move. And a dark mist was closing round her.

Someone hissed out a muffled curse. It wasn't her so she had to presume it must be him, though she was way too distressed to be absolutely sure of that. The next moment two hands were grasping her shoulders and lifting her to her feet. The stack of documents slid to the floor forgotten as he wrapped her tightly in his arms.

And suddenly she felt as if she was under attack from

a completely different source. Attack—why attack? she asked herself as her head became filled with the warm solid strength of him.

'Oh, my God.' She groaned.

'What's happening?' he muttered thickly.

'I d-don't know,' she said tremulously, and tried sucking in a deep breath of air in an effort to compose herself. That deep breath of air went permeating through her system, taking the spicy scent of him along with it, and in the next moment her brain cells went utterly haywire.

Familiar. That scent was familiar. And so wretchedly familiar that—

Once again she fainted. No more warning than that. She just went limp in his arms and knew nothing for long seconds.

This time when she came round she wasn't lying but sitting, with him standing over her pressing her head down between her knees with a very determined hand.

'Stay there,' he gritted when she tried to sit up. 'Just wait a moment until the blood has had a chance to make it back to your head.'

She stayed, limp and utterly exhausted, taking in some carefully controlled breaths of air while she waited, waited for...

Nothing, she realised. No bright blinding flood of beautiful memories. Not even ugly ones. Nothing.

Carefully she tried to move, and this time he allowed her to, his dark face decidedly guarded as she sat back and looked at him.

'What?' he demanded jerkily when she didn't say a word.

Empty-eyed, she shook her head. She knew what he

was thinking, knew what he was expecting. She had been expecting the same thing herself.

His dark eyes glinted, a white line of tension imprinting itself around his mouth. Then he sucked in a deep lungful of air and held onto it for a long time before he let it out again.

'Well, we aren't going to try that again,' he decided. 'Not until we've consulted an expert to find out why you faint every time you're confronted with yourself.'

Not myself, she wanted to correct him. *You.*

But she didn't, didn't want to get into that one. Not now, when it felt as if her whole world was balancing precariously on the edge of a great, yawning precipice.

'So that settles it,' he declared in the same determined tone. 'You're coming with me.' He bent down to pick up the scattered papers, his lean body lithe and graceful even while it was clearly tense. 'I'm going to need to make a few phone calls,' he said as he straightened, then really surprised her by dropping the photograph back onto her lap. 'While I do that, you can go and pack your things. By then I should be finished and we can get on our way—'

'Do I have any say in this at all?' she asked cuttingly.

'No.' He swung round to show her a look of grim resolve. 'Not a damned thing. I've spent the last twelve months alternately thinking you were dead and wishing you were dead. But you aren't either, are you, Samantha?' he challenged bluntly. 'You're existing in some kind of limbo land to which I know for a fact that only I have the key to set you free. And until you are set free, I won't know which of my alternatives I really prefer, and you won't know why you prefer to stay in limbo. The newspaper report on you said they took you to a hospital in Exeter after the accident, which I presume means you received all your treatment there?'

She nodded.

So did he. 'Then, since Exeter is where we are going, we don't mention the past or anything to do with the past until we've received some advice from someone who knows what they're talking about.' He settled the matter decisively. 'All you have to do is accept that I am your husband and you are my wife. The rest will have to wait.'

CHAPTER FOUR

WAIT...

Carla certainly did think she should *wait* for answers before trotting meekly off with him. 'But you don't know him from Adam!' she protested as Samantha moved around her room gathering her few possessions together. 'How do you know if he's telling the truth?'

'Why should he lie?' Samantha countered, turning the question round on itself.

'I don't know.' Carla sighed in frustration. 'It just doesn't *feel* right to me that you are willing to go off with him without knowing what it is you're going to!'

Samantha's only answer was to silently hand Carla the wedding photograph.

She stared at it, then at Samantha, then back at the photo again. And suddenly her mood changed. 'What can have happened to you to make you forget something as beautiful as this?' she murmured painfully.

Samantha wished she had the answer to that one. The story that photo was telling might be bringing tears to Carla's eyes, but she couldn't even begin to describe how it made her feel.

Nothing, she named it. But it was a strange, pained nothing, which was, in itself, something terribly saddening. 'Do you know who he is?' she asked quietly.

'Nathan Payne told me.' Carla nodded. 'But just because he's the great Visconte himself doesn't absolve him from having to explain why it's taken him twelve months to come and get you!'

True, Samantha conceded, and sat down on the bed as the heavy weight of all her own uncertainties came thundering down on her again.

'I mean...' Carla went on, determined to push her point home now that she had Samantha wavering '...you were famous for a week or two in these parts when the accident happened. Your predicament was reported in all the local papers. If you were missing and he was worried about you, wouldn't you expect a man like him to pull out all the stops in an effort to find you? At the very least he could have checked out the police stations and hospitals. Your looks are pretty damned distinctive, Sam,' she pointed out. 'Even without you knowing who you are, for someone to be searching for a tall, slender redhead going by the name Samantha would surely be enough to make the necessary link?'

'Maybe he was away—out of the country or something,' she suggested, thinking of New York.

'You mean, you haven't bothered to ask him?' Carla sounded dismayed.

Samantha was a little dismayed herself at how little she had asked him to explain. But the truth of it was, she didn't want to ask. In some incomprehensible way, it felt safer not to ask.

'The trouble is,' she admitted with a rueful grimace, 'every time we discuss anything even vaguely personal, I faint.'

'Even more reason, surely, for you to think carefully before putting yourself in his care. Don't you see that?'

See it? Of course she did. But...

Easing herself back to her feet, she gently took back the photograph, then looked at Carla with disturbingly bleak yet resolute green eyes. 'If I am ever to discover why I've ended up like this,' she said quietly, 'then I have to go with him.'

To her, it was as simple and as final as that.

Where was she? André flicked a hard glance at his watch then stuffed his hand back into his pocket. She was taking an age!

'Damn,' he muttered, feeling the hellish anger he had been keeping banked down take another step closer to exploding. 'Look at this place,' he growled out contemptuously. 'If it fell down right now, no one would miss it.'

Nathan Payne looked up, and André suddenly saw himself as his manager was seeing him—like a prowling panther pacing up and down on the awful carpet in front of the reception desk, as if in need of a good fight.

Hell, he thought. Ten rounds with the best boxer in the world wouldn't knock out the ugly stuff churning up his system right now.

Samantha, residing in these miserable surroundings. It was enough to snuff the living light out of anyone! And the sooner he got her away from here the better as far as he was concerned.

Where was she? 'Ring her room,' he instructed Nathan.

'No,' the other man refused. 'She will come when she's ready.'

'She's already been an hour.'

And that other girl was with her. She didn't like him. He'd seen it in her face when she'd heard what Samantha was going to do. She thought he was being too pushy and that Samantha was in too deep a state of shock to be going anywhere with anyone. Damn it, she was right, he grimly conceded.

'Don't you think you are being a bit hasty, taking her away from the only secure environment she knows?' Nathan posed levelly.

Don't you start, André thought. 'I can give her a secure environment,' he insisted.

'She's in shock, André.'

'So am I,' he tossed back.

'And she's frightened.'

Did Nathan think he didn't know that? 'I'm not into S&M, Nathan,' he rounded angrily on the other man. 'I'm not going to chain her up in a cage and put a whip to her rear end every hour on the hour!'

'I'm so very relieved to hear that,' another voice inserted.

Spinning round, he saw her standing in the mouth of the corridor which led to the staff quarters. She was wearing a simple blue shift dress and her hair was still fixed in a dreadful, priggish bun, which was in itself a defiance of what the real Samantha was. Deliberate, or a subconscious act? he mused grimly, and felt his senses grind together. Deliberate or not, it was there. Her chin was up, her mouth small, and her eyes were tossing out the kind of cold green sparks that had always declared war—old Samantha style.

He had never been able to resist it, and didn't even try. Relaxing the tension out of his body, he let his eyes send back a counter-declaration, and he taunted lazily, 'Submission is not your forte, *mia dolce amante*. You demand equality in all aspects of your life.'

He threw in the 'my sweet lover' in Italian just to see if she would remember it; he saw her face grow pink and was very, very pleased that she did indeed understand what he'd said. Standing beside her, he also saw her friend shift uncomfortably. Behind him he felt his manager do the same. He didn't actually blame either of them, because sexual tension was suddenly rife in the dull and dingy foyer.

But it was Samantha's response that mattered to him, and as the first truly healthy one he'd managed to rouse in her it did his bad temper the world of good.

'Are you ready to come with me?' he tagged on silkily, deciding to build on his sensual success—a building that crumbled the moment she moved forward and he saw that she was using a walking stick.

Anger roared back to life, making him turn on Nathan like a rattlesnake with poison dripping from its fangs. He snapped out orders which Nathan took in his stride with a kind of silent sympathy that only helped to make him feel worse. But he couldn't even begin to describe what it did to him seeing his beautiful, vibrant Samantha in so much pain that she needed help just to walk!

Samantha left him to it and went outside, hurt by the flare of dismay she had seen on his face when he'd caught sight of her walking stick. Nor did she like the autocratic way he'd spoken to Nathan Payne, whom it seemed was going to remain here and cover for Samantha until the hotel manager returned.

'He's a bully,' Carla said.

Samantha couldn't deny it so she remained silent instead.

'And he fancies the hell out of you,' Carla added.

Static electricity suddenly shivered through her, setting almost every hair she possessed on end. 'Not this girl,' she denied, giving the walking stick a deriding kick.

'What was the Italian seduction scene about, then?'

'You said it.' Samantha shrugged. 'The words "Italian"

and "seduction" always go together. In fact I don't think they can function without each other.'

'So he's an Italian-American.' Carla assumed.

Samantha shrugged again, because she didn't actually know. Certainly the Visconte name was Italian. The accent was most definitely American, but the first name was surely French? she mused frowningly.

'Are you going to be all right?' From being argumentative, Carla had seen the frown and was now sounding anxious again.

No, I don't think I am going to be all right, she thought, staring bleakly out across the potholed car park to where two cars in particular stood out like the symbols of success they obviously were. One was a natty black Porsche, the other a racing-green Jaguar.

'Samantha—?' Carla prompted her for an answer.

She gave one. 'I'm not *all right* as I am now,' she pointed out. There didn't seem anything left to say after that.

André came striding out of the hotel, and the atmosphere suddenly took on a distinct change. Reaching out, Samantha took her suitcase from Carla, who had insisted on carrying it for her this far.

The two girls hugged while he looked on—or 'glared' would have been a better word—a set of keys jingling impatiently in his hands as he did so.

'Take care of yourself,' she murmured to Carla as she drew away.

'No, you take care of you,' Carla returned.

'Let's go,' his hard voice said.

Samantha felt the old panic erupt inside her and had to work very hard at damping it back down. As he set off down the hotel steps the sun came out, giving his skin an extra warmth that added a luxurious sheen to it.

'Call me,' Carla begged as a final farewell.

'I promise.' She nodded, and felt a burn begin behind her eyes as she took that first mammoth step to follow him.

Maybe he sensed the tears. Certainly something made him pause and look back. Eyes like black marble lanced over her. Samantha lowered her own eyes and bit down on her bottom lip, fought hard to concentrate on negotiating the steps instead of the wave of anguish that was trying to overwhelm her.

His hand snaked out. She hadn't even realised he'd moved back towards her until she felt the suitcase being taken from her. Then, without another glance at anyone, he strode off towards the Jaguar, opened the boot, threw the case in, then went round to open the passenger door to stand beside it like a jailer waiting to lock his latest prisoner in.

Which made her think of cages and chains, which in turn almost caused a hysterical bubble of laughter to burst in her throat. Swallowing both tears and laughter, she kept her face turned away as she reached the car and lowered herself into it.

Without a by-your-leave, her stick was taken from her. The door shut with a very expensive thud, and she found herself experiencing a different kind of luxury, made up of soft cream leather and walnut veneer. Five seconds later his door came open and he was bending inside to toss her stick onto the car's rear seat. She caught the tantalising scent of his skin as he folded his long body in the seat beside her. He had put his jacket back on but his tie still hung loose around his throat. He looked lean and mean and decidedly alien.

Without a single word being spoken between them, he pulled his seat belt across his wide chest and locked it in place, glanced briefly her way to check that she had already done the same. Then, with a final settling of his long frame, he started the engine, shoved it into 'drive', and swept them away.

It was all so swift, she decided, so final. As she caught her last glimpse of the hotel, she felt the tears burning the backs of her eyes once again. Goodbye, she lamented silently—then wondered why she felt as if she'd said goodbye like this to some other run-down, dearly loved building?

'Why the stick?' he bit out suddenly.

'If my limp offends you,' she flashed at him coldly, 'then maybe you should turn around and put me back where you found me. Because the limp it isn't going to go away just because you don't like it!'

'It doesn't offend me,' he denied. 'It makes me bloody angry, but it does not offend me.'

She wished she believed him but she didn't, and it didn't help that it had to be her scarred profile he saw every time he flicked a brief glance at her!

'Tell me about it,' he persisted stubbornly.

Does he never give up? Taking a deep breath, she gave him what he wanted. 'The knee was crushed in the accident but the injury was made worse by the urgency with which they had to pull me from my car before it went up in flames.' He winced, but she didn't care; he'd asked for this! 'I've since had four operations on it and, believe it or not, the limp is not half as obvious as it was two months ago.'

With sarcasm abounding in that last comment, still he didn't give up. 'Any more operations to come?'

'No,' she replied. 'What you see now is what you get. So if you were hoping to recover the same person you see in that photograph you gave me, then let me tell you

now, before this thing goes any further, that you won't
be getting her!'

'I'll be getting the temper, though, I notice,' he
drawled, and was suddenly smiling, smiling in a way
that made her heart flip over. Smiling with his eyes and
a genuine amusement that completely altered his face.
He was smiling at her as if she'd just given him some
special present instead of yelling at him like a harridan.

'Keep your eyes on the road!' she cried as a desperate
diversion away from the emotions that were suddenly
churning up her insides.

He began to curse, shocking her with the abrupt way
he took his foot off the accelerator and turned his attention back to the stretch of curving Tarmac in front of
them. 'I'm sorry. I didn't think. Obviously you will be
nervous about being in a car after—'

'No.' She sighed, feeling just a bit guilty for making
him think that she was. 'Not so long as the driver is
competent—which you clearly are.'

At which point another silence fell, while he made
himself concentrate on his driving and Samantha's mind
went lurching off on an agenda of its own.

'So, tell me why the Tremount Hotel has been left to
fall into such a miserable state,' he invited after a minute
or two. 'It looked as if it must have been quite something
once upon a time.'

'It was,' Samantha agreed, relieved to be given a more
neutral subject to fill in the silence while they travelled.
'Victorian,' she said. 'Originally built to accommodate
the upper echelons of British middle-class society of its
time. And filled with some real architectural treasures if
the right person knew where to look for them.'

'They would have to look hard.' André grunted.

'They would have to possess *soul*,' Samantha corrected, forcing André to respond with a rueful grimace at her set-down. 'It fell on hard times when the British holiday market shifted abroad. But now the market is coming back to its own shores places like the Tremount could have a lot of potential for the right developer. It has its own beach, and isn't too far away from the nearest resort town. Also, there is a large piece of land to the right of the main building you may have noticed as you came down the driveway. It was once a nine-hole golf course until it was left to fall into disrepair along with the hotel. With the right expert on the job, it could…'

André let her talk on, harshly aware she had no idea she was giving him a report on the hotel's potential that was as detailed and informed as any of his top surveyors could offer him. But, then, Samantha couldn't remember, and therefore had no idea that this kind of thing came as second nature to her. Or that, like himself, she had been involved in the hotel industry all of her life.

Nor was she aware that she was interspersing her words with his name, just as she'd used to do. And her hands—always the most busy tool she used to express herself—were motioning and measuring, long fingers pointing, marking, making those delicate circling movements with a twist of her slender wrists that were so familiar to him.

It made him want to hit something. Because the sensual sound of his name falling from her lips and the hand movements might belong to the old Samantha, but nothing else about her did. Not the priggish hairstyle, nor the dowdy clothes, nor the expression in her eyes—which should be animated while she talked but was as dull and flat as the tone of her voice.

The old Samantha was a vivid bright fireball of energy. This one was shocking him by her stillness, her lack of passion for anything—if you didn't count the moments they'd touched on the subject of their marriage. Then she'd revealed passion all right, he acknowledged grimly. A passionate horror that had had her fainting clean away.

It took over an hour to reach Exeter. But Samantha had been talking so much that she was surprised when the car came to a smooth halt in the forecourt of a hotel.

'So this is the famous Visconte Exeter,' she observed curiously. 'I remember reading in the newspapers about its big gala opening last year—'

Last year, she then repeated to herself, and began to frown as a sudden thought struck her. 'Did you come to the opening?' she asked sharply, the very idea that he could have been this close to her without either of them knowing it hurting her for some unexplainable reason.

Something in his stillness grabbed her attention. His eyes were hooded and his jaw line clenched. He answered her question, 'No.' And then he got out of the car to swing round the long bonnet so he could open her door for her.

'Why weren't you here?' she demanded instantly.

He began to frown. 'I don't understand the question.'

Her eyes flicked up, green and hard. 'Why weren't you here to attend the opening of your own hotel?' She spelled it out succinctly.

'Good grief.' He laughed, but it was a very forced laugh. 'I don't attend every opening we have.' Reaching down, he unfastened her seat belt since she had not got round to doing it herself. 'The Visconte chain stretches right around the world. I would have to be Superman to—'

'You weren't even in the country, were you?' Samantha cut in.

She could remember it now. The big party to celebrate the opening. The coverage it had received in local newspapers because of all the big-name local celebrities that had attended. My God, she'd had little else to do as she'd lain imprisoned in her hospital bed than pore hungrily over every article written in them.

Searching. She had been searching for something that might have jogged her memory. But it hadn't happened.

Why hadn't it happened? How could she have not even recognised her own married name when she'd read it so often?

Because she'd blocked it out, she realised painfully. Just as she'd blocked out everything else about this man until he'd come along today and had virtually force-fed the Visconte name to her.

So she could also remember the papers remarking on the fact that the owner himself had been expected to attend the opening but had pulled out at the last moment—because he'd been out of the country on other business.

Out of the country barely a month after her accident.

Her eyes lanced him with a bitter look. 'Did you bother trying to look for me at all?' she asked coldly. 'Or was our marriage already over by the time I disappeared?'

His face closed up tight. 'I'm not going to answer any of that,' he said, taking a firm grip on her arm.

'Why not?' she challenged, resisting his tug. 'Because the answer may paint you as less than the caring man you would like me to believe?'

'Because the answer may have you fainting on me

again,' he corrected. 'And, until we seek professional advice on that problem, we don't talk about us.'

With that, he firmly propelled her out of the car, then released a soft curse when he saw her bite down on her full lip as she placed her weight on her injured leg.

Having to concentrate hard not to cry out, Samantha grabbed hold of his arm for support. Once again her senses went utterly haywire, and she found herself standing there, not only having to brace herself against the pain, but having to brace herself against the feel of tensile muscles flexing beneath her grip. He was all power and hard masculinity, she likened hazily, watching images build in her mind of warm dark golden flesh and a disturbingly attractive sexuality that somehow merged with the physical pain she was experiencing until she couldn't distinguish one sensation from the other.

'Just how painful is the damned thing?' he rasped out angrily.

It stole the moment—stole a whole lot more—when she opened her eyes and found herself looking at a man who was *still* a stranger. And as she stood there, held caught in a sea of confusion, the physical pain separated itself from painful imagery like two lovers untangling, then became only a hard, tight, aching throb that completely obliterated the other.

Green, André was thinking. Her eyes were so green— a dark and pulsing passionate green colour they had only used to go when they were making love. But today there was something else there, confusion and pain and a terrible despair that made him want to hit something again.

'Answer me,' he commanded, aware that the violent emotions flailing around inside him had everything to do with the expression he had seen burning in her eyes.

'Damn painful,' she replied, lowering her gaze to

watch as she carefully bent and straightened the knee a couple of times before trying to stand on it again.

And he was glad that she had looked away. Much longer having to witness her expression was likely to have finished him. It had been hard enough controlling the urge to pull her into his arms and just kiss the pain away for her.

Not the wisest course of action to take when the woman in question had the clever knack of falling into a deep faint if he so much as touched on intimacy. He grimaced, clenched his jaw firmly shut, and watched in grim silence as she placed her foot on the ground then carefully transferred her weight onto it. This time it remained there, and the grip on his arm slackened. She released a sigh, then let go of his arm altogether.

'Okay,' she said. 'If you could just pass me my stick…'

It was like moving from a rock to a very hard place. No sooner had he managed to contain one set of angry emotions than another set erupted inside him. This new set having something to do with that damn stick and his fierce resentment of it.

'You will lean on me,' he determined.

'Not while I still have another alternative.' She hit back with throbbing venom.

'My God.' His breath left his lungs on a hiss of impatience. 'Why do you insist on seeing me as some kind of monster?'

She flushed, not with guilt but with anger. 'You were already out of this country within a month of my disappearance,' she charged. 'How else am I supposed to translate that?'

He refused to answer, withdrawing from the fight by flattening his mouth into a tight line as he shifted his attention away from her and with a snap of his fingers brought a blue-liveried doorman running.

End of discussion, she noted angrily, listening to him snapping out instructions to the doorman about her suitcase before he leaned past her to retrieve her stick. In grim silence he offered it to her and in grim silence she took it. Then in the same grim silence they began walking towards the hotel entrance—together but separate, like two polite strangers, with her challenge still hanging in the air between them like an omen of whatever was to follow.

CHAPTER FIVE

THE hotel interior was more or less what she had expected for a deluxe-class establishment. No garish splashes of yellow on purple here, but a soft blend of creams and greens, which contrasted beautifully with a subtle placing of a dark wine-red colour, set against the kind of unashamed luxury which made an absolute mockery of what they had just come from.

Though the quality of her surroundings was the last thing on her mind when, only a few minutes later, she found herself standing inside a suite of rooms with this man and at last began to feel the vulnerability of her situation.

Maybe he was beginning to realise the same thing, because he released a small sigh, then turned to face her. 'Okay?' he asked guardedly.

No, she wanted to reply. I'm not okay and I want to go back where I came from. But common sense, or stupidity—she wasn't sure which—stopped the words from coming.

'You've already been using this suite,' she remarked instead, having noticed the signs of habitation in the few personal items she could see scattered about.

'I arrived late last night,' he confirmed, 'in time to come up here and sleep off some of my jet lag before I came to find you.'

The late London train, as Freddie had suggested, Samantha realised, and smiled a little wryly as she turned away from him to pretend to take an interest in her surroundings—mainly because she couldn't think of another thing to say.

Another silence formed. She sensed him watching her as she moved around the suite, opening doors and closing them again before moving on to the next one.

'Found what you're looking for?' he enquired eventually, though he was sardonically aware of what it was, she was sure.

Well, the suite comprised two bedrooms with their own *en suites*, she confirmed. So there was no need to fight for her privacy. 'Yes,' she said—and diverted her attention to the view beyond the window, with her chin up and her green eyes definitely telling him he could mock her all he liked.

The telephone began to ring then. Samantha was never so relieved to hear the sound. While he strode over to a desk standing at the other end of the room, she reached for the handle and opened a French window that led out onto a large, private balcony. Stepping outside, she walked over to lean on the balcony rail and, after a tense little sigh, allowed herself the luxury of a few deep breaths of fresh air, only realising as she did so that it had been a long time since she'd breathed in and out properly.

Stress, tension. Tension, stress. Was there a difference between the two of them? she wondered bleakly, and decided that even if there was a difference the two had become one tight sensation to her.

Oh, why did I let myself be talked into coming away with him like this? Samantha asked herself, as the full weight of her own vulnerability tumbled down upon her head.

Then, You know why, she told herself grimly. He

knows who you are. He's the man who holds the key to all of your problems.

Or is *he* my problem? she then suggested, and felt a cold chill touch her flesh, as if fate itself was offering her an answer. She was married to him, she'd seen firm proof of that, so why didn't she *feel* married? Glancing down at her left hand, she saw no sign that a ring had ever resided there.

So, where was her ring? If she'd been wearing one at the time of the accident, it certainly hadn't been on her finger after the crash.

'I have to go out.'

His deep voice coming from behind her made her turn warily. He was standing, propping up the opening, studying her through heavily lashed hooded dark eyes. His hair was short and neat and black and he wore his clothes with a casual ease that belied their sophistication. Nothing wrong with his body, nothing wrong with his face. So what was it about him that she found so upsetting? She gave her own answer. The inner man. The inner man worries you; the outer one simply disturbs you.

'Business,' he explained, making her blink her eyes into focus on him. 'I should be back in a couple of hours. But I've ordered some lunch for you. Then I suggest you take a rest.' His black lashes flickered as he ran his gaze over the way she was leaning so heavily on the stick. 'Nathan said you spend every evening standing behind the bar at the Tremount; was that wise considering how weak that knee actually is?'

'The knee is fine so long as I pace myself,' she answered coolly.

He ignored what she had said. 'All night serving behind a bar. All day working behind a reception desk. It's no wonder you look so worn out.'

Her chin came up, green eyes beginning to burn with resentment. 'I have to eat, like anyone else.' She said it almost accusingly. He noted it with a sudden darkening of the eyes. 'And I liked my job,' she added. 'I will always be grateful to the manager of the Tremount for taking me on, considering how—worn out I look and how many hours I had to take off to attend the necessary hospital appointments. He was good to me.'

He rejected all of that deridingly. 'You were good to him, you mean. Neither of you knew it, but he was lucky enough to acquire one of the most experienced hotel executives in the game when he took you on.'

She was surprised to hear him say that—yet not surprised when she considered how naturally she had seemed to fall into hotel routine. It probably should have occurred to her sooner that she might have worked in the trade before.

'And the need to worry about where your next meal is coming from,' he went on flatly as he levered himself away from the door, 'is now well and truly over.' He eyed her critically. 'And priority number one, once I've dealt with this bit of—business, is to get you fitted out with some decent clothes. You're used to luxury, not tat. Samantha,' he said.

'Anything else about me which doesn't meet with your approval?' she mocked, stung.

'Yes.' His eyes began to glint. 'The way you're wearing your hair. It makes you look like a toffee-nosed prude when I know for a fact you're an absolute witch. It isn't fair to give wrong impressions about oneself to others. It means they fall into nasty little traps they can't get out of.'

'Is all of that supposed to imply something specific?' she demanded, stiffening at his criticism.

'Of course,' he drawled. 'But that's for me to keep to myself and you to find out for yourself.' Then he straightened. ' Now I'm off,' he announced. 'I'll be back as soon as I—'

'You said I don't have to worry about eating again,' she cut in, anger simmering nicely now. 'Does that mean I have you to rely on for food, or do I have money of my own stashed away somewhere?'

'You have a very healthy bank account,' he informed her, naming one of the big high street banks.

'So all I have to do is walk into one of the branches and prove who I am to get at my own money?' He confirmed it. She smiled. 'Then, watch out, *signore*,' she responded—acid-sweet. 'Because if I am the witch you call me, I may just decide to disappear on you for a second time. I wonder if you'll experience a sense of *déjà vu* if I do?'

He was standing in front of her before the last word had trailed into taunting silence. 'Just try it.' He growled. 'And this time I promise you I'll follow you to the ends of the earth if I have to!'

She defied the warning burning in his eyes. 'Why didn't you the first time?'

'Where is your evidence to say that I didn't?' He challenged her right back.

'You were out of this country barely a month after I disappeared; that says a lot, don't you think?'

'I was out of the country. Yes,' he hissed back at her. 'But why I was out of the country is just one more question you're going to have to search that—' reaching up he pressed a fingertip to her temple '—closed mind of yours to find the answer to.'

Her reaction managed to shock the pair of them. She shrank back from him so urgently that she almost toppled over. 'What was that for?' He snarled, automatically reaching out to steady her.

Once again she pulled away. 'I h-hate it when you touch me,' she choked with an awful little shudder.

His eyes went black, a furious anger suddenly flaring on the sting of her insult. 'Hate?' He flicked the word at her in a thin silken tone that had her throat closing over. 'Well, let's just try this as a little exercise to test the strength of this so called hatred—'

And the next thing she knew she was being held fast by a pair of angry hands and his mouth was against her mouth. Her senses went into a complete tail-spin, sending shock waves ricocheting through her body as the most horrendous feeling of familiarity completely overwhelmed her.

She knew this mouth. She knew its feel and its shape and its sensual mobility as it coaxed her own mouth to respond. His tongue ran a caress along the line of her tightly closed lips and she recognised the light, moist gesture as his way of making her open up and welcome him.

But, worse than that, she wanted to. She wanted to respond so much that she began to whimper, having to fight herself as well as the kiss as sensation after frighteningly familiar sensation went clamouring through her system. Heat began to pool deep down in her abdomen, desire licked a taunting flick across her breasts.

It was too much. She couldn't bear it.

Her stick hit the balcony floor with a hard clatter as her hands snapped up to push him away. But they didn't push, they clung to his shoulders. And she was being assailed by yet more hot waves of familiarity. She knew his height against her own height. She knew his width and the superior power in his much stronger body.

And she knew the pleasure in feeling small and frail and oh, so feminine when held against him like this.

Maybe he sensed it. Maybe he was reading her body language. Because his hands shifted from her shoulders and began to smooth their way down her back to her slender waist. She groaned as he drew her hard up against him because—God help her—she let him do it.

Let his lips crush her own apart and let their tongues make contact and let him taste her and simply surrendered the battle to this hot and seductive taste of passion.

He withdrew. It was so abrupt that she just stood there, leaning against his hard-packed framework staring up at him in blank incomprehension.

'Yes...' he hissed down at her in soft-voiced triumph. 'You might think you hate my touch, *cara mia*, but you cannot get enough of my kisses. What does that say about what is happening in here?' he posed, bringing the whole, wild episode back to where it had started by tapping a finger against her brow again.

And just like that the familiarity disappeared and she found herself looking at a complete stranger. A cruelly taunting stranger with eyes still glinting with a residual anger and a mouth that still pulsed from the damning kiss. It was no wonder she shuddered again.

'Also, no faint,' he mocked, adding insult to injury by stepping right back from her in a way designed to mockingly prove that she was indeed still conscious.

'You bastard,' she breathed.

His lazy shrug conveyed a complete indifference to the title. Then he turned and walked gracefully towards the window. 'See you in a couple of hours,' he said to accompany his careless departure. 'And make sure you take that rest. You look like you need it.'

Samantha simply stared after him, too deeply sunk into a slow-dawning understanding to know or even care what he'd said. He had kissed her in anger. It had been a punishment as well as a demonstration of his power over her.

'I'm to blame, aren't I?'

The shaky claim brought his feet to a standstill.

'I did something so unforgivable that I daren't let myself remember.'

'No,' he denied.

She didn't believe him. It had to be her fault or why else had he treated her as he had just now?

'Apportioning blame will not help the issue,' he added grimly.

'Then, what will?'

He shook his head. 'We agreed not to discuss the past until we'd sought professional advice.'

Her short laugh scorned that remark. 'That's rich coming from the man who's just imposed the past on me with about as much ruthlessness as he could muster!'

'All right!' he rasped, reeling round to catch her off guard again. She jumped as if frightened. His teeth showed white in angry acknowledgement. 'That,' he said, waving a hand at her reaction, 'is why I kissed you! Why I was angry—why I still am! We were lovers, Samantha!' And suddenly he was striding towards her again. Hands reaching up. Hands grabbing her shoulders. 'Hot, greedy, *passionate* lovers, who never could get enough of each other! So of course it damn well infuriates me when you jump if I so much as come near you! Being near you and *not* kissing you means I am denying myself—as if it isn't enough to have one of us doing that! So—' He bent, kissed her once more, like a terse punctuation. 'Get used to it. You're my wife. I like kissing you. Now I'm getting the hell out of here before I decide to convert all of this anger into something else I like doing with you!'

And with that he turned and strode away, leaving her standing there feeling shell-shocked and shaken by the barrage of emotion he had just thrown at her.

The suite's outer door closed with a controlled slam. She blinked, breathed, and only realised when she did it that she hadn't drawn breath throughout his last angry speech. Her lips were still burning from the power of his kiss and her body was trembling so badly she began to wonder if now was going to be the moment that she sank into a faint.

It didn't happen. Instead she managed to take a step forward—and tripped over her walking stick as she did. The trip jarred her knee and, wincing, she let fly with a few choice curses as she rubbed the offending joint and fervently wished she had never set eyes on André Visconte!

'Ever,' she tagged on fiercely to that wish.

André was standing in the hotel manager's office, shooting orders down the telephone as if he was conducting a bloody war.

It was late, and he'd just come away from an interview at the police road accident department which had left him feeling turned inside out. Guilt was devouring him, along with agony and distress and a blinding black fury that was threatening to swallow him whole.

'Just do it!' he growled out at Nathan when he dared to argue the point. 'If Samantha says it has the potential, then at least do her the honour of accepting that she knows what she's talking about!'

Nathan began to patiently explain that it wasn't Samantha's word he was questioning, but the wiseness of André making such a big corporate decision feeling as wound up as he did.

'Do *you* think the Tremount has potential?' André questioned coldly.

'Yes,' Nathan replied. 'But—'

'Then what the hell is it you're arguing about? Set up the damn deal and just let me know how much it's going to cost me.'

'For Samantha?' Nathan drawled.

'Yes!' he hissed back. 'It's for Samantha! And while you're at it, make sure that friend of hers—Chrissy—is taken care of.'

'Carla,' Nathan corrected.

'Carla, then!' he all but snarled. He wasn't in the mood for all of this. 'Put her on our payroll. Samantha worries about her.' And anything—*anything* Samantha worried about had to be eliminated!

Samantha...

'Hell,' he muttered, and slammed down the receiver, then slumped back against the desk to bury his face in hands that were shaking.

Now he'd seen the photographs he couldn't get them out of his head. The roadside carnage. The twisted wreck of burnt out metal that said more clearly than words what had happened to her.

Then there were the other pictures, ones that came without photographs but were still just as gruellingly graphic, of her waking up in some strange hospital, suffering from shock and pain and a total disorientation with the strange world around her.

And where had he been while all of this was happening?

Halfway round the world on a bloody wild-goose chase!

Now she was sitting upstairs, no doubt waiting for him to continue where he had left off earlier.

Imposing himself on her. Staking his claim. He shuddered and despised himself. He wouldn't blame her if she'd taken up her own threat and had made another bolt for it.

Oh, dear God. Had she—?

Dragging his hands away from his face, he looked down at his watch to find he had been gone for almost three hours instead of the two he'd told her he would be.

With a jolt, he sprang forward and made for the door in a hurry. Samantha could disappear into thin air with a few hours to do it in. He should know; he'd had previous experience. The lift took him upwards. He paused outside their suite and took a few moments to smooth out his wrecked emotions before slotting in the access key and quietly opening the door...

CHAPTER SIX

THE suite wore an air of hushed quietness. It chilled his blood—until his eyes alighted on Samantha. She was lying asleep on one of the soft cream sofas, looking as if she had been there for a long time.

Slowly he walked towards her, his footsteps silenced by thick green carpet. The lunch he'd had sent up still sat untouched on the table by the window. He frowned, then deepened the frown when he saw two packs of tablets sitting beside the lunch tray.

Picking them up, he read the labels. One lot of tablets he recognised as the named-brand painkillers she had taken earlier. But he felt his gut squeeze in dismay when he recognised the other as a famous-brand tranquilliser.

Had she taken these? Had she taken *all* of these? Had he finally managed to drive her into—

His head shot up and round, his eyes locking onto her in a moment of skin-crawling horror.

Then, No, he grimly calmed himself. She wouldn't be that stupid.

But he found himself checking out the pack and almost sinking to the floor in relief when he discovered none of the tranquillisers missing. Going to squat down beside her, he gazed into her sleeping face. She still looked pale, but some of the strain had eased away.

As if she was able to sense the very moment he came within touching distance, her eyes suddenly flicked open and he found himself gazing into sleepy green.

'Hi.' He greeted her softly, aware that he was already on his guard, ready to field a hostile response.

It didn't come. Instead she simply lay there looking at him as if she was searching for something she needed to see.

Remorse for his earlier behaviour? he wondered. Well, she had it. 'Sorry things got a bit out of hand before,' he quietly apologised. 'Believe or not—' he grimaced '—I am finding this situation as difficult as you must be.'

'I understand.' She nodded, then seemed to realise that she was staring and broke the eye contact by sitting and sliding her feet to the floor.

It was his cue to move away, and he did so, having no wish to give her reason to erect her defences yet again. Straightening up, he looked around him for something neutral to say. 'You didn't eat your lunch.' It was all he could come up with.

'I wasn't hungry,' she replied, leaning forward to stroke exploring fingers across her damaged knee.

'How is it?'

'Better.' She showed him by flexing it with an ease he hadn't seen before. 'I took some anti-inflammatories, then fell asleep while I was waiting for them to work. What time is it?'

André glanced at his watch. 'Five-thirty.'

She nodded and stood up. He was really surprised by the lack of stiffness in her movements. It was almost like the Samantha he used to know.

But that Samantha wasn't really here, he grimly reminded himself.

Her polite voice intruded. 'Did your meeting go okay?'

'Fine,' he said, then turned his back on her, grabbed

the back of his neck and just stood there staring into space while his mind played back a reel of still frames that would look great in a horror movie.

What was he thinking while he stood there like that? Samantha wondered warily. He'd seemed all right. The anger had gone, so too the desire to shock her into reacting. Yet he clearly wasn't comfortable with what had replaced it. Something must be bothering him or he wouldn't be standing there looking like a man at a loss to know what to do next.

'Are you all right?' she asked him reluctantly, not wanting to provoke a return of their earlier hostilities.

He released an oddly muffled laugh. 'Actually, no,' he said, then turned to wing a rueful smile at her. 'I came back here half expecting to find you'd carried out your threat and made a bolt for it.'

If he'd meant to make her smile, she didn't even come close to it. 'Where would I go?' she asked him bleakly. 'You may think I like being like this but I don't,' she added. 'I need to find out about myself and, as you rightly pointed out to me, you seem to be the only person who can help me do that.'

'I don't think anything of the kind about you.' He sighed. 'I don't doubt for one minute that you must be afraid of what all of this must mean.'

'Were we...?' she stopped, changing her mind.

'What?' he prompted.

'Doesn't matter.' She shook her head.

'You're going that dreadful shade of grey again,' he informed her levelly.

'I'm okay,' she said and discovered that it was her turn to turn away from him. 'I think I'll take a shower...'

'Good idea,' he agreed. 'I think I will do the same.'

Relief quavered through the atmosphere, put there because each was glad of the excuse to escape the other. 'My room is the one on the left,' he told her. 'They are both more or less the same, but if you want to swap I don't—'

'The one on the right will be fine,' she cut in, and began to limp towards it with no sign of the nagging pain. It was amazing what a couple of pills could do Samantha mused wryly.

'Food,' he said suddenly. 'We both need to eat. Let's make it an early dinner,' he decided. 'Say, seven o'clock?'

Samantha nodded in agreement, too eager to escape, now that she had an excuse, to start up a discussion on whether she could swallow a single morsel as her throat felt so tight.

'Seven it is, then,' he confirmed. 'I'll book a table in the restaurant. Unless you would rather eat up here?'

'No,' she said quickly. 'The restaurant will be fine.' The last thing she wanted was to be incarcerated in this suite of rooms with him for a whole evening. 'I...'

'What?' he prompted when she carefully severed yet another sentence.

She shook her head, aware of the explosive properties in dryly promising not to show him up by stepping out with him wearing polyester. 'I'll see you later,' she murmured, and found her escape in the bedroom she had already claimed as her own by unpacking her suitcase and hanging up her few clothes.

André watched the door close behind her and at last released the tense sigh he had been holding in check. This wary truce they had managed to achieve was harder to deal with than the constant lightning bolts they'd been delivering across each other's bows.

Would it last?

No, it wouldn't last, he acknowledged ruefully. She might be different, but she was still Samantha. A fiery temperament was as much a part of her nature as it was a part of his own. It was the reason why they'd fought so much, loved so much and, in the end, almost destroyed each other.

Well, not this time, he vowed as he moved across the room towards his own bedroom door. Samantha might not understand this yet, but the two of them had been given a second chance and this time they were going to use it wisely.

He was going to use it wisely, he then amended. Because he couldn't expect Samantha to be wise after an event she didn't even remember.

At precisely seven o'clock Samantha took a final look at herself in the mirror, drew in a deep breath, then walked towards the door, reasonably confident that he was going to be feeling quietly relieved when he saw how she was dressed.

For, despite his derogatory impression that her clothes were tat, she had a dress. A very expensive matt-black crêpe cocktail dress, kindly donated to her, among other items, by the wife of one of her doctors who'd taken pity on her—and who'd also gone up a couple of sizes since she'd bought the clothes.

Most of the other stuff she'd had replaced with new just as soon as she could afford to. But this dress had been too good to let go so she'd kept it, never really believing she'd ever get a chance to wear it.

But here she was, doing exactly that, and not only did she think the dress looked good on her but it also *felt* good in the way the beautiful fabric moved against her slender shape. She had washed her hair with the expensive toiletries in the bathroom, and had discovered that you truly did get what you paid for because, as she'd blow-dried her hair, it had been a pleasurable experience to watch the colour become more vibrant the drier it had become.

So she'd left it to fall free around her shoulders— mainly because she suspected he was expecting her to screw it up in defiance of his toffee-nosed prude remark. Also, she had applied some make-up, paying careful attention to the strained bruising around her eyes. The only thing letting her down were the low-heeled black court shoes she was forced to wear.

But otherwise she was ready to be seen out in public with him, she told herself firmly, and lifted her chin and opened the door.

André was already there, standing over by the desk with one hand braced on it as he leaned over some papers. He looked quite painfully gorgeous.

And he was wearing a plain white tee shirt, grey linen trousers—and that was it.

While she had been dressing up he had been dressing down, and the realisation almost shattered her carefully constructed composure.

Then he looked up, saw her standing there, went perfectly still, and her composure shattered anyway. For this man wasn't just breathtakingly attractive, he was dangerously so. Black silk hair, olive-toned skin, eyes like bitter chocolate which seemed to melt as they moved with an excruciating slowness from the top of her head to the shoes on her feet. His facial bone structure was perfect, his mouth essentially male, and the muscular configuration beneath that tight white tee shirt screamed sex at her—*sex*.

Slowly he began to straighten his torso, the hand sliding away from the desk the more upright he became. But what really took her breath away was the way his eyes gentled as they made contact with her own eyes.

He knew. He knew she was feeling at a loss to know how to deal with the obvious crossed wires in the communication. Yet all he said was, 'A punctual woman, and a beautiful one too.'

Then, reaching out to close the manila file, he picked it up and said lightly, 'Hang on just five seconds while I put this away, then we will go and eat...'

Stepping into his own room, he *was* only five seconds. But he still came out wearing a grey linen jacket that completely transformed him from a mere casual diner to a stunningly chic one.

Only a man with Italian blood running in his veins could have done it. Only a man with a great deal of sensitivity could have pulled it off with such quiet aplomb.

She was impressed. She was grateful. She was seduced. He won her full attention by hypnotising her with his deep-toned, smooth, sexy, American accent, and with the quick smile that would suddenly flash out, adding a dangerous charm to an already dangerously attractive face.

They shared a table for two in a corner of the restaurant, where they talked quietly about innocuous things, like food and wine and the leisure industry. His concentration on her and whatever she had to say was so intense that she felt it like a constant buzz of awareness from fingertips to head. His eyes never left her. And his well-shaped mouth was firm but edged with a sensuousness that persistently reminded her of that kiss.

A kiss she had known. A kiss she had enjoyed. A kiss she had responded to without having to think. Even now, as she sat here watching that mouth move as he talked, she could feel its pleasurable pressure burning against her lips.

Attraction. She was aware of a physical attraction pulsing softly in her blood. She liked it. She was beginning to like him. Samantha started to relax, lower her guard, and even caught herself laughing once or twice.

Then he ruined it by picking up his glass of blood-red wine, swirling it round in thoughtful silence for a second or two, and saying levelly, 'I have a confession to make.'

Her eyes leapt to his, the green softened by what had been happening to her sharpening into instant wariness. His mouth went awry, as if in acknowledgement that he was about to spoil what had so far turned out to be a perfect evening.

'When I said I had to go out on business this afternoon I allowed you to assume it was hotel business, but it wasn't,' he explained. 'What I actually did was spend some time with your doctor.'

Her coffee cup rattled as she put in back on its saucer. 'Why would you want to go and do something like that without me there?' she protested.

'Because I had some very sensitive things to tell him and I felt they would be better said without you there to hear them.'

'About me,' she presumed, her soft mouth tightening to hide a deep stab of hurt.

'About the both of us,' he said, making it clear.

Her eyes flashed with resentment. 'He isn't supposed to discuss me with anyone!' she said tightly, feeling hunted suddenly, strangely, frighteningly, *angrily* hunted.

'He didn't. He just listened while I talked, then advised me on the best course to take with this problem we have.'

This problem, Samantha repeated to herself. How good of him to let me know what I am. 'And his advice was what?' she prompted coldly.

'That we take it very easy from here on in,' he replied, watching her, his eyes never leaving her face for a moment. 'He agrees with me that your memory is not buried quite so deep as you assume it to be. Your reaction to me is enough to substantiate that. But he advises no brutal question-and-answer sessions. No intense probing, but to allow things to come out in a slow, natural everyday way because he thinks the fainting thing is worrying. So we have to tread very carefully if we are not to cause further problems. And he wants to see you before we go back to London. He—'

'London?' she interrupted. 'Who said anything about me going to London?'

'I did,' he said. 'It's where we live. Or one of the places we live, at any rate,' he wryly amended. 'I have a branch office there. We have a house. He suggests we go there and try to pick up the threads of our normal life so that you can—'

'What normal life?' she countered tautly. 'What is even vaguely normal about me going to London with a man I don't remember, to a house I don't remember, to a life I don't remember?'

'What is normal about *not* remembering?'

Her face froze over, her awareness that he was only speaking the truth filling her with her own sense of helplessness. But she hated him for making her feel that she had no right to direct her own life because she didn't have a functioning brain in her head!

'If, between you, you've both already decided on

what's best for me, then why does he want to see me at all?' Her voice throbbed with resentment.

He did not respond to it. 'He feels you may need—reassurance that I mean you no harm,' he explained.

'Really? Does that include some reassurance that he has my best interests at heart also?' Her green eyes flashed him a look of scorn. 'Well, forgive me for not seeing things that way!'

'Why are you so angry?' he questioned curiously.

If she didn't get out of here she was going to toss the last of her wine in his face. 'Because you went behind my back and discussed my situation without my agreement,' she sliced at him. 'And if that isn't devious, I don't know what is! And to make it all worse, *he* actually let you get away with it!' She could barely breathe she was so infuriated by that!

'I needed advice and he needed to be in possession of all the facts before he could offer me that advice.' The arrogant devil was shrugging it all off, as if his answer justified what he had done.

And it did in one way, Samantha conceded. But it certainly did not in another. 'You could have lied through your teeth to him for all he knows!'

'I told him the truth,' he stated quietly.

'So everyone knows the truth about Samantha but Samantha. How cosy,' she derided, and got to her feet.

'Running away again, darling?' he taunted dryly.

She didn't bother to reply—didn't want to, actually. Did not damn well want to! she told herself fiercely as she walked away.

And she did it without a hint of a limp, André grimly noted as he watched her go. She would probably pay for that bit of pride in the morning, he predicted.

Ignoring looks from their fellow diners, who had been

keeping a curious eye on them from the moment the altercation had begun, he hissed out a tense sigh, thinking, So much for believing there was safety in numbers. Then he lifted his glass to his lips to swallow what was left of the red wine before getting up to go after her.

As he had known she would be, she was standing by the suite door, bristling with frustration because she didn't have the means to let herself in so that she could complete her angry exit by shutting herself away in her room before he could get to her.

And he grimly wished she had been able to do that—not for his sake but for her sake. Because her inability to get into the suite without his help was just another example of how out of control of her own life she must be feeling right now.

And she was trembling, he realised as soon as he came up beside her and silently fitted the card into the slot. Stiff-backed, chin up, eyes staring fiercely ahead—but trembling like a fine slender leaf having to fight against the wind that was trying to blow her away.

'Samantha—'

'Don't speak to me,' she cut in, walking through the door the moment he released the locking mechanism.

He followed her inside, closed the door, and watched her stalk stiffly across the room and shut herself away.

Maybe that wasn't a bad thing, he told himself as a real bone-weariness began to pull at him. It had been a long and gruelling day for the both of them, and he was still suffering the remains of jet lag. A night's cooling-off period might do them both a bit of good, he decided. And, with a little bit of luck, by the morning she might be seeing the sense in what he'd done.

Not that he held out much hope of that, he then admitted with a grimace that was half a smile. Because he knew Samantha, even if she didn't know herself. She was hot and she was stubborn. And he was in for a battle.

A battle he fully intended to win. For there was no room to back down now. No going back. And the sooner Samantha came to terms with that, the better it was going to be for both of them.

CHAPTER SEVEN

HE WAS half right on most counts, André discovered the next morning when she appeared for breakfast wearing a dusky mauve outfit consisting of a skimpy camisole-type top and a tight little skirt in a darker shade of mauve. Both of which did hot things to his libido even though her icy demeanour was supposed to be freezing out all of that.

Her hair was back in its screwed-up knot, and she was limping again. It didn't surprise him but it damn well annoyed him. Would she ever learn to embrace caution?

No, he answered his own question. Caution had never been a word Samantha recognised.

'I'll keep that appointment,' she announced as she joined him at the table.

It was all he was going to get, and wisely he didn't try for any more, other than murmuring a relaxed toned, 'Coffee's hot, juice is cold, take your pick.' Then he returned his attention to the newspaper he had folded open on the table.

As for Samantha, she refused to react to his non-reaction, though she was pretty sure he was sitting there expecting her to. And even if he did look good this morning, in a bright white shirt and grey silk tie that matched the colour of the jacket hanging on the back of his chair, she still hated him and still fiercely resented the way he was orchestrating her life.

It was a resentment which hadn't faded one little bit

by the time she stepped out of the specialist's consulting room a couple of hours later.

She found André lounging on the corner of the desk belonging to the pretty receptionist, who was looking all smiling and doe-eyed at him.

The little flirt, she thought scathingly. And worse—he was enjoying it! Resentment turned into something really ugly that burned like acid in her chest.

'If you're ready,' she snapped with enough venom to make them both take note of the green sparking in her eyes.

The nurse blushed, but he didn't. In fact his eyes began to gleam behind the dangerous slits he had narrowed them into. Samantha ignored the both of them and walked as haughtily as she could with a limp towards the exit door, felt him come up behind her and had to fight to suppress the urge to spin round and scratch his flirting eyes out!

'Watch it.' The warning was spoken in silken threat right against her earlobe—and suddenly she froze like a statue as a desperate sensation of *déjà vu* went washing through her.

Sensing the change, he stepped around her so he could look into her face before releasing a soft curse and grimly taking hold of her shoulders. 'You've gone that funny shade of pale again,' he informed her huskily.

'Mr Visconte?' The receptionist's voice was pitched with fluttering concern. 'Is your wife feeling ill? Shall I—?'

'Just get me out of here,' Samantha breathed tautly. 'I need some fresh air.'

Without another word he folded an arm across her shoulders to lend support while murmuring a polite goodbye as they made their exit. As soon as they were outside, Samantha moved right away from him. She felt hot and stifled, and had to stand gulping in some much needed breaths of air in an effort to stave off the feelings of faintness while he watched and waited for her to get a hold of herself again.

'Well,' he said finally, 'are you going to tell me what brought it on this time?'

No, I am not, she answered silently. 'It was just too warm in there, that's all.'

'Liar,' he drawled. 'You were about to faint again and we both know it.'

Her colour returned—all her hostility returning right along with it. 'Do we really have to have an inquisition on every small gesture I make?' she flicked at him.

'No.' He shrugged, displaying a frustrating calmness the more irate she became. 'But if you feel fit to spit, I assume you also feel fit to walk?'

'Go to hell,' she said, and limped off down the shallow steps and onto the street.

He fell into step beside her, not touching but close enough to catch her if she decided to fall into a pathetic swoon.

They reached the car. He unlocked the door and saw her inside before going around to climb in beside her. The engine fired but the car didn't move. Sitting there beside him, staring fixedly ahead, she waited with gritted teeth for what was coming.

As if on cue, the first question arrived. 'What did the doctor say?'

'Exactly what you said he would say,' she replied. '"Be a good girl. Do as you're told and everything will be fine one day."'

Her tone dripped sarcasm. But she couldn't help it,

she felt as if she were fighting for her very life here—yet she did not understand why!

Again, he showed that uncanny knack of latching onto her thoughts by sighing heavily. 'Why do you feel you have to do battle against me all the time? Did the doctor offer you no reassurance at all about me?'

'He performed beautifully,' she assured him. 'He confirmed that you are indeed who you say you are and I am who you say I am. He then went on to ask me a lot of questions which I have to *presume* were supposed to give everyone else answers to what is wrong with me—since everyone seems intent on keeping me in the dark about myself! Then he went on to advise me to work *with* you not *against* you, because you only had my best interests at heart.'

'But you don't believe that?' he assumed from her acid tone.

'What right do I have to an opinion?' She laughed thickly. 'I'm just the headcase who can't trust a thing her instincts tell her!'

'And what are your instincts telling you about me?'

'They're telling me that for some reason, known only to you and your new friend my doctor back there, you are about to manipulate me to suit your own purposes!'

'In what way?' He wasn't angry, just curious—which only managed to infuriate her further, because she saw analysis in every question he asked her—just like the doctor.

'I tell you what.' At last she turned to lance him with a look. 'I'll make a deal with you. For every answer I give you, I get one back.'

He studied the glint of challenge in her eyes for a long moment; while she sat there, wishing he was as ugly as sin because it would make it so much easier to keep him at a distance then. But he wasn't ugly, he was beautiful, and her throat closed up on a block of tears because she wanted so much to reach out and touch him.

Touch him, taste him, lose herself in him so she didn't have to think, fight, worry whether or not he was a man she could place her trust in when she couldn't even trust herself to know what was right.

'Okay,' he quietly agreed. 'Ask.'

It wasn't the answer she had been expecting. It threw her into turmoil. Sucking in a tense breath, she held onto it as panic began to build with enough power to burst through her skin. Then she said, 'No.' She breathed out like a deflating balloon.

'Because you don't want to know the answers or because you don't feel ready to know?'

'Because I'm sick and tired of the whole stupid subject!' she cried, filling with hot, pressured air again. 'It's boring! You're boring! I've lost my memory, okay?' she tossed tightly at him. 'I don't know you, and for all I do know you could be some raving sex maniac I had to run away from or get devoured!'

He laughed! He had the outright gall to laugh out loud. 'If there are any sex-mad fiends lurking in this car then they're sitting in the other seat to mine,' he said dryly.

'That's an absolute lie!' She gasped, going prickly hot all over at the very suggestion that she could be like that!

For an answer he leaned across the gap separating them and kissed her. She ignited like brushwood as all those angry emotions running riot inside her swiftly converted themselves into something else entirely, and before she knew it her hand was claiming the back of his head in her urgency to keep his mouth joined with hers.

It was she who compelled their lips to open, she who hungrily deepened the kiss. And it was she who groaned with agonising pleasure when he let her do it all.

And it was also she who shrivelled up with shame when it had to be him who broke the heated engagement. Point well and truly made.

She was surprised when he said nothing but instead merely repositioned himself in his seat and set them moving with a smoothness that utterly belied the tension still sparking between them.

Sex-mad, she repeated to herself, and shivered. Could her brain be suppressing the shame of being raving sex-mad? Dragging her eyes away from him, she fixed them straight ahead and struggled very hard not to suffocate in a sense of self-loathing.

Bringing the car to a halt outside the main doors, he climbed out then came around to her side of the car to watch her alight. His jaw clenched as she paused to exercise the knee a little before trying to walk on it. But he said not a word, didn't attempt to offer help, and even Samantha was surprised when she reached out to place her hand on his arm as they began moving.

Hard muscle flexed again. She tried to ignore the effect it had on her. If she had any effect at all on him, then he ignored it too. Neither spoke; they just walked, hand to arm as couples do.

But as they walked through the hotel entrance he stopped, then muttered a couple of rich curses beneath his breath.

'Listen,' he said, 'you aren't going to like this, and I know I don't, but there is someone standing at the reception desk we both know.'

'Who...where?' she said, hunting the busy foyer at

the same time as a shaft of nervous tension straightened her spine.

'His name is Stefan Reece, and he's talking to a receptionist right on the end of the desk.'

She saw a tall man with fine blond hair and what looked like an easy smile, chatting pleasantly with the receptionist. Warily she moved a little closer to André's big frame. He responded by twisting round until he was half blocking her from view.

'Now, don't get jumpy,' he chided. 'He's a competitor, that's all.' And he named a hotel chain that she instantly recognised, before going on. 'He'll be here scouting. We all do it—check out the competition to see if they're offering a better service than we are offering ourselves. Since he's already seen us, we can't avoid him,' he added with a clip to his voice that said he wished otherwise. 'But it's up to you how we deal with this. We can pretend there's nothing wrong, exchange a few pleasantries, then get the hell away from him before he realises there's something different about you. Or we can keep to the truth and get into the complications of trying to explain it all.'

Which told her exactly which option he preferred and, frankly, so did she. In fact the very idea of trying to explain she couldn't remember her own name made her feel distinctly nauseous.

'He'll see the limp,' she said. 'And the scar...' Instinctively her hand jerked up to cover the side of her face.

Lifting his hand, André took hold of her hand and firmly lowered it to her side again. 'Stop it,' he scolded. 'The scar is barely noticeable except in your mind.'

'I haven't got a mind, remember?' she gibed. 'And he'll know that too the moment he speaks to me!'

'It's your memory you've lost, not your wits.' He sighed in exasperation. 'All you need to do is smile a reasonably convincing smile, and leave the talking to me. You can do that, can't you?'

Could she?

'André—Samantha!' a deep voice greeted. 'This is a pleasant surprise!'

Speak for yourself, Samantha thought childishly.

'Maybe a bigger one for us than it must be for you?' André suggested dryly as he took the other man's out-stretched hand.

'Caught red-handed in the enemy camp.' Stefan Reece admitted it. 'What can I say? Unless I remind you that the boot was well and truly on the other foot the last time I saw you.' He grinned. 'Sydney, about a year ago if my memory serves me right. And you were checking out my establishment—but without this lovely creature along with you to make my day. Hello Samantha,' he murmured warmly, offering his hand to her next. 'You're looking as beautiful as ever, I see.'

'Thank you,' she said. If he'd noticed the scar he hid it well, she thought, and was grateful enough to find an answering smile. His laughing eyes darkened; it took him longer than it should have to release her hand again. And she felt the man standing beside her give a restless shift.

'How's business?' André asked, and it was so near to an angry rasp that she glanced sharply at him.

'Good—though not as good as you seem to be having it,' Stefan Reece was saying ruefully. 'Which reminds me.' He then turned to Samantha, his face lighting up. 'I went by the Bressingham the other day, expecting it to be open by now, but...'

Samantha had stopped listening. The name

Bressingham name had tugged at a chord somewhere deep down inside her, and she was suddenly experiencing such an overwhelming sense of grief that she could barely cope with the power of it. Her heart began to throb so slowly and thickly that her fingernails coiled into taut male flesh without her even being aware whose waist it was she was clinging to.

'Have you just arrived, Stefan?' The harsh rasp of André's voice sliced through whatever it was that was holding her.

The other man blinked, glanced quickly from one tense face to the other and seemed to realise he had made some huge blunder here, though for the life of him he didn't know what it was. 'Just checking in when I saw you two standing here, so I...'

'Then let me make sure they give you the best available suite. On the house, of course.' With a snap of his fingers André brought a hotel attendant running. With only a few terse instructions he had Stefan Reece settled in one of the best suites, and the arm he had resting across Samantha's shoulders had turned into a crushing anchor.

'It would have been nice if we could have had dinner together tonight, but Samantha and I are leaving for London this afternoon, and...'

So soon? The information was just another shock Samantha had difficulty coming to terms with.

'Shame,' Stefan Reece was saying. 'It isn't often we get a chance to...'

Her mind kept shutting off, she realised. Concentrating on full sentences seemed completely beyond her scope. She kept hearing the word 'Bressingham, Bressingham'. It hurt but she didn't know why it hurt.

The arm about her shoulders urged her into movement. She complied as if through a floating haze within which she could hear the two men talking. Yet she wasn't there with them. It was a strange experience, walking, hearing, yet feeling many miles away.

'*Cara*, Stefan is saying goodbye to you,' a voice prompted softly.

'Oh,' she said, and blinked but couldn't' focus. 'Goodbye, Stefan. It was nice to see you again.' The words arrived automatically. His reply was lost in the resuming haze.

The next thing she knew, she was standing in the lift being transported upwards and André was standing over her, literally propping her up against the lift wall.

'You don't have to do that,' she protested. 'I can manage on my own now, thank you.'

He moved away but she could tell he didn't want to. And all he did was move as far as to lean a shoulder against the wall right beside her. He was concerned, she could feel it, yet he didn't attempt to ask her what had brought the faint feeling on this time.

'You don't seem to have managed very well over the last year without me,' he murmured huskily instead. 'In fact, I would go as far as to say you've made one hell of a mess of trying to manage on your own.' And, to make his point, his hand came up, gently touching the puckered scar at her temple.

She reacted by flinching away from his touch so violently, this time, that she banged the other side of her face on the lift wall.

'You bloody fool!' he exploded. 'What did you think I was going to do to you?'

'Just don't touch me like that again!' she choked out,

green eyes flaring with bitterness. 'I hate you! I don't
know why I hate you but I really, really hate you!'

'You're overreacting.' He sighed.

'M-maybe,' she conceded. 'But...'

But what? she asked herself helplessly. You *are* overreacting to a lot of things! Overreacting to a consultation
with a doctor which was, in reality, the most common
sense thing to have done in the circumstances.
Overreacting to a kiss that shouldn't have happened but
did *and* you enjoyed it! Then you overreact to the prospect of meeting someone you should know but don't
and, to top it all off, you really overreact to a name you
do know but cannot work out why!

'Bressingham,' she said huskily. 'What is the
Bressingham?'

'Why?' He sounded about as uncooperative now as
she knew she had been sounding since he'd stridden
back into her life.

'Because I recognise it from somewhere but I can't
remember where.'

'Story of your life.'

The lift stopped, the doors sliding open to allow two
people to come in, stalling Samantha's desire to retaliate
to that one.

So they smiled politely at the polite smiles they received, then stood stiffly beside each other while the lift
continued on its way up. And the tension in the small
confines of the lift was fraught—so fraught the other
couple kept glancing warily at each other. And by the
time the lift ejected the intruders on the next floor
Samantha was beginning to wonder if her throat would
ever open up again.

The doors closed and up they went again, with the
same taut silence accompanying them. Another stop, and

this time he stretched his arm out to hold back the doors in an indication that they had reached their floor.

Reluctantly Samantha limped forward. As she went to go by him, he stopped her with a clipped, tart, 'You don't hate me, Samantha. You just wish that you did.'

For some reason—she didn't know why—her hand snaked out and caught him a stinging slap across his face.

For what felt like a full minute afterwards, both just stood there staring at the other, her with a pain and hurt and anger she just could not comprehend, he with a black fury that said he was having to stand stock still like that or retaliate in some way.

Having just enough sense left to err on the side of caution, she turned and walked away. But once again she found herself having to wait for him to open the suite door for her, and she was trembling by the time that he did so.

Once again she took the direct route to her bedroom the moment she got inside, and once again André watched her make her escape while telling himself to just to let it go—while the feel of her fingers still stung his cheek.

Only this time he found he just couldn't leave it. This time he refused to be shut out by a closed door. Anger, pride, stupidity, you name it, he found he wasn't going to give himself time to think about his next action as he strode grimly after her.

CHAPTER EIGHT

SAMANTHA was standing in the middle of the room, desperately trying to justify what she had just done, when the door suddenly shot open.

Her heart began to thump somewhere in the region of her stomach. He was angry and she didn't blame him. Her fingermarks were still lying like an accusation against the side of his face. Remorse pushed her into speech.

'I'm sorry,' she said immediately. 'I didn't mean to do it. I don't know what came over me.'

He didn't even acknowledge the apology. The door closed with the help of his foot. The room was suddenly filled with the scent of danger. His eyes were black and his mouth hard. A warning chill went slinking down her spine. I've managed to set the devil loose, she realised uneasily, and decided that this could well be a good time to faint.

But she didn't feel in the least bit faint. In fact she felt disturbingly—

'N-no,' she stammered out, lifting up a trembling hand meant to ward him off as he began striding towards her. 'Stay there. Let me try and explain...'

He just kept on coming. It was like being stalked by an angry predator. Fear and an unexpected excitement began to war in her blood. He came to a stop a hair's breadth from her outstretched, trembling fingers. She saw it as a reprieve and rushed back into speech again. 'It-It's been a d-difficult twenty-four hours for me,' she

explained unsteadily. 'I w-was overwrought, n-not thinking straight. I just—snapped. I didn't want to, but—'

'Well, guess who else has snapped?' he posed, caught
the outstretched hand and used it to pull her towards
him.

The softness of her breasts made impact with solid,
male muscle. It was like making contact with pure electricity; a static charge lit up nerve ends so fiercely that
she could actually hear them crackle. She tried to pull
away but it was already too late; his other arm had
snaked around her waist to hold her firmly against him.
Even as she released a protesting gasp, his dark head
was lowering.

Oh, she tried to fight him. She twisted and turned and
went through a series of denying groans and quivers—
and kissed him back as if she couldn't get enough of
him. It was awful. She was appalled at herself, yet her
mouth clung hungrily and her body writhed closer to the
uncompromising hardness of his.

Because she wanted this. Wanted what she knew was
going to happen with the need of a woman who had
been waiting for this moment for much too long.

Too long…she repeated, and knew it was the truth.
Too long hurting, too long wanting, and too long waiting
for this man to come to her.

It was a knowledge which had another sob clutching
at her throat. He felt it and lifted his head to look down
at her. He was still angry. She could see it glinting in
his eyes. She could see the passion too, the flame of
desire that, angry or not, he couldn't manage to hide.
'You've vented your filthy temper on me many times,
cara,' he told her thinly. 'But you've never raised your
hand to me before.'

'I'm sorry,' she said again, but it was a different kind

of sorry. It was low and soft and unbelievably sensual—
and spoken as she was twisting her fingers free from his
so she could gently lay them against the marks she had
placed on his face.

His eyes began to burn. Hers darkened in a dramatic
surrender to what it was she knew she wanted here. The
hand moved on, fingers sliding into his silk black hair
and around his nape—before pulling his mouth back to
hers.

'You bloody hypocrite,' she heard him breathe as they
resumed that vital contact.

He was right, and she was. But it didn't stop the pair
of them from enjoying a sensual feeding frenzy with
frantic deep kisses and restless hands that touched and
stroked and acknowledged no boundaries in their quest
to taste the whole banquet.

It was hot and it was hungry. Samantha didn't know
herself, the touch of his stroking hands and the passion
in his kisses seeming to draw a completely different person out of her skin: a wild and wanton person with a
throbbing, pulsing sensuality that demanded full attention and made sure she got it. Where he touched, she
revelled in sheer, luxuriating pleasure. Where he didn't
she writhed in restless demand.

He muttered something into her mouth she recognised
as a signal to tone the whole thing down. But, no way,
she thought feverishly, and ripped shirt buttons from
their holes so she could place her hands against the hair-
roughened beauty of burning, tight flesh. All hint of ton-
ing anything down faded in that moment as, with a deep
shudder, he took back control by running his hands beneath her top. Dragging her mouth from his, she released
a soft, shivering gasp as pleasure went singing along her
skin where he began to caress her.

'You don't know what it is you're inviting here,' he growled darkly.

I do, she thought. 'Don't talk,' she commanded, terrified that speech was going to break the magic spell surrounding them.

Instantly his mood flipped back over, the moist tip of his tongue stabbing at her lips in an insistent command for her to part them again. When she did, he began to torment with short, slick, sensual forays into her mouth that made her light up inside.

This was the point where he began to seduce her in earnest, Samantha recognised from somewhere within the turmoil. His hands caressed, his mouth seduced, and her clothes began disappearing. She didn't care—in fact she welcomed their loss. He stroked her breasts, her back, the soft pink curve of her bottom. When she sighed out in pleasure, he rewarded the sigh with deep probing kisses to keep her submerged in a world of pure sensation.

When he decided to lift her up and carry her to the bed, her eyes came open to reveal the green, darkened by desire but alive to what was actually happening.

'What?' he questioned very softly. His tone was a measured seduction in itself. Laying her down, he came to lie beside her, leaning close to her pulsing lips to murmur, 'Tell me what you want and I will give it to you.'

He was speaking in Italian, low and hushed and intensely intimate. When she merely lay there and listened, with her eyes dark and vulnerable, he said gently, 'Do you want this to stop now?'

He meant it too. If she told him yes, she wanted it to stop, he would move away without a single protest. But it never even became an issue. Gazing deep into the desire darkened depths of his eyes, 'No,' she whispered.

He rewarded her with another long, soul-stripping kiss. But it was also a softly seducing, beautiful kiss. And it didn't stop there. He began to kiss her all over. He kissed her chin, her nose, the flickering lids hiding away her eyes. He slid that devastatingly skilled tongue-tip around the small scar at her temple. The gesture filled her with the most incredibly sweet sense of loving.

But when she began to caress him he stopped her with a silken, 'No,' and firmly returned her hand to the mattress.

It was his seduction, and he was determined to play it his way, she realised. And she just lay there and let him. Why? Because she wanted to be seduced. She wanted to simply lie here and feel—feel anything and everything he could possibly make her feel.

When his kiss began trailing down her throat she groaned as he paused, then bit sensually into the pulse-point leaping there. The feel of his mouth closing around one erect pink nipple lost her the last dregs of conscious reality. Her flesh was alive and demanding total concentration, the smallest brush with his mouth set a million nerve ends shimmering.

I know this, she found herself thinking hazily. I've been here before, been reduced to this beautiful state of boneless pleasure many, many times before. I know this man. I know his touch. I know what's coming, which is why I daren't so much as breathe in case I distract him.

This was living at its most sensual. When his tongue began slowly circling her navel, sensation fanned out in a heart-stopping ripple, followed almost instantly by an overwhelming stillness as a knowing finger made sliding contact with the very core of her sexuality, centering all that concentration on the one area as desire swelled, then burst like a flower opening up to the life-nourishing heat of the sun.

'André.' She sighed, and he felt the thick drug of power surge in his body.

This woman was *his*. Mine, he thought possessively, every sigh, every pleasurable quiver, every silk-smooth, sensual cell that made up her beautiful body. Even her thoughts—her damned hidden thoughts—belonged to him while he touched her like this.

But it wasn't enough. He wanted more. He wanted everything, he decided as the power of his own burgeoning desire grew too strong for him to contain any longer. Breaking free, he came to his feet beside the bed, saw her eyes flicker open in bewildered surprise then wince shut again as a shaft of afternoon sunlight struck into them.

In a single stride he had closed the curtains, diffusing the light in the room to a seductive softness, before turning back to find her eyes open again. Without a word, he began stripping his clothes off while she lay there half on her side, and saying not a word to try to stop this.

But then they were still making love—with their eyes and his body movements—and the way she lay there, following the removal of each piece of clothing with such devotion, flooded each newly revealed part of his compact muscle-structure with a burning sense of masculine arrogance.

'You study me with the curiosity of a virgin,' he murmured as he came to lie beside her.

She just smiled a bewitchingly provocative smile, and in the next moment he rolled her onto her back and punished the smile with a kiss that changed the whole tempo of what he had been creating before.

Samantha placed her hands on his body and this time he didn't attempt to stop her. Each touch became a deliberate torment, heightening the senses to a pitch that was almost savage in their quest to wring the most from the other. She stroked his arms, his back, dug her nails deep into the flesh which formed his lean, tight buttocks, and his teeth grazed tauntingly across a nipple then hungrily drew the whole stinging areola into his mouth.

And hot—he was hot. His skin was hot, his mouth—the moisture within it. She drew in a tight breath of air and found the scent of his body so intoxicatingly hot it turned the air to a thick, smooth, sensual steam she was reluctant to breathe out again.

When he came back to plunder her mouth, she responded by closing her arms around him and flattening her body up against his body, breast to breast, hips to hips—soft pulsing sex making contact with hard probing sex. He rolled with her until she was lying on top of him, her kissing him, her moving on him, her hair—having escaped from its knot long ago—tumbling in a silken trail of spiralling waves all around his face and shoulders.

Then her knee began to protest at the uncomfortable pressure she was placing upon it and, on a tiny groan, it was she who was changing their position, rolling onto the mattress beside him and trying to bring him with her. But he was too shrewd for his own good. He'd heard the groan and had recognised it for what it was. Before she realised what he was doing he was leaning down to kiss the hairline pink scars which criss-crossed the once smooth and perfect area.

'No,' she whimpered, strangely upset by what he was

doing, and she reached to grasp a fistful of his hair to pull him away again.

He let her do it, but came to lean over her with a face carved with tension. 'If you *ever* put your life at risk again, I will personally kill you!' he rasped at her furiously.

She still held tight to a fistful of his hair, and in reply she brought his mouth onto hers to kiss away the fear raking through him. And it *was* fear; she knew that instinctively. It filled her with a most peculiar feeling of warmth tinged with aching despair.

And, as if he knew it, he entered her like a man caught between two kinds of hell. It should have hurt it was so fierce and possessive. But it didn't hurt. It was in fact the most exquisite sensation she felt she had ever experienced. He thrust deep and she welcomed him like a long-lost, desperately missed lover.

'André,' she breathed again.

It sent him spinning over that finely balanced edge between control and sexual insanity. He drove into her like a man who was being given his last chance to experience this level of ecstasy. And she took each hot, lancing thrust with gasps of pleasure, growing shrill the closer she came to reaching the goal he was driving her towards.

Yet when she reached it she went quiet, and his hand trembled when it raked up to push the tendrils of hair away from her face, so he could watch this woman, who did everything with such frightening totality, absorbing each consuming wave of pleasure he was inducing, in a silence that pierced his heart with the knowledge that she was no longer of this world but floating on another plane entirely.

Then he joined her. With one more sweet, slow

plunge, his eyes drew closed and his features grew sharp as he began to spill out his own fierce pleasure.

Neither of them was aware of anything much for the next few, communal minutes while they made a slow return to a sanity that seemed more exhausting than the climb out of it.

Then he became conscious of his weight pressing heavily down on her and reluctantly decided to move. His careful withdrawal from her body caused a final mutual spasm of residual pleasure, then cool air touched their sweat-sheened flesh as he rolled onto his back beside her on the bed.

After that they just lay there, with eyes closed and bodies slack, waiting for reality to come filtering back in. It was the calm after the storm with another storm hovering in the near distance, threatening to roll in depending on what they both chose to do or say next.

Eventually he turned, moving onto his side to face her, and touched her cheek with a finger. 'Okay?' he asked huskily.

Samantha nodded, and though her eyes flickered open she couldn't seem to bring herself to look at him, so she stared at the ceiling instead while she admitted sombrely, 'I knew your touch.'

The finger stilled in its gentle tracing of her cheekbone. Reaching up, she caught the finger, clutching at it hard as she added shakily, 'I knew you.'

He didn't try to recover the finger. In fact he didn't do anything but lie very still. 'You say *knew* not *know*,' he remarked finally. 'Is that significant?'

She closed her eyes again, nodded and felt a tear creep out from the far corner of each eye. 'Nothing else,' she whispered. 'I just—know your touch, and for a while I knew you...'

Which was why she was gripping his finger so tightly, André pondered grimly to himself. And wanted to cry with her, it was that damned wretched.

'I'm so afraid it will be all I'll ever know now.'

On a sigh he gathered her in, kissed her brow, stroked his cheek over her tumbled hair, and left his finger right where it was, because—hell—if she did need to touch him then let her keep the finger! He didn't need it. But, God, he needed her.

'It will be okay.' He tried to sound reassuring, though he was no more certain of anything than she was herself. 'Trust me, *cara*, and I will promise to get you through this as quickly and as painlessly as I can.'

'It will be painful, then?'

'Yes.' He sighed; it was no use denying it. It was, after all, why they were supposed to be taking things so carefully.

And why they should not even be here like this.

Fool, he cursed himself. A ban on intimacy to this degree should have been a foregone conclusion to anyone with intelligence. Keep your hands off until you have a right to touch, he'd told himself, because he was acutely aware that he had lost that right twelve months ago. So what had he done? Within twenty-four hours of setting eyes on her again he'd tumbled her into the nearest bed and taken just about every liberty he could with her.

Well done, André, he mocked himself harshly. At least last time you managed to wait a whole week before you took her to bed. This time you could barely manage a full day.

Well not again, he vowed. Not until she recovered every last wretched memory! Then he almost groaned in frustration when she began absently stroking the tip of

his finger over the softness of her lips. His body quickened. He shut his eyes and grimly forced his senses back
into the cupboard they had been languishing in for a
whole, miserable year.

'Come on,' he said, and got off the bed then bent
down to lift her to her feet. Already he was getting used
to waiting patiently while she used his forearms as support until she gained a reasonable balance.

'Okay?' he prompted when her grip slackened.

'Mmm,' she said.

Looking down to check for himself that she was indeed managing before he took his arms away, he saw
long and slender naked flesh, pearly white skin and a
cluster of fine ginger curls, which reminded him of certain sensual pleasures he still hadn't reacquainted himself with... Then he had to turn away before she could
see what was happening to him.

'Right, go and have a quick shower, then pack your
things while I do the same,' he instructed briskly, striding around the room to pick up his clothes. 'I would like
to leave here within the hour if we can do it.'

'We're still leaving today?'

Her tone alone was enough to have him straighten,
with his final piece of clothing, to see her still standing
where he had left her, looking like a beautiful Titian
goddess, wearing a lost and frightened expression on her
face that cut him to the quick.

She didn't want to leave Devon and what she had
come to feel safe with. And he had no choice but to
insist they leave, because her past was in London—and
his future, if she was going to let him have one once
she recovered her memory, that was.

'Of course,' he said.

'London,' she murmured, and he hated to see that vulnerable expression hollowing out her lovely green eyes. It was impossible not to respond to it, and on a sigh he walked back to her, kissed her once, firmly.

'Home,' he corrected firmly. 'We are going home...'

CHAPTER NINE

THEY were an hour into their journey before either of them spoke more than a few frustratingly short syllables without a protective coating of politeness on their voices.

Home, he'd said, and instantly the barriers had gone back up between them. He'd erected his wall, Samantha suspected, because he wasn't going to change his mind and didn't want to argue about it. She had put her wall up because she wanted to argue but didn't seem to have any grounds to do so.

Home was home. Of course he wanted to take her back there, she reasoned. Or why else would he go to all this trouble to come and get her? Home probably also held a million clues as to why she was like this, and if she wanted to recover her memory then home was the most logical place to go and look for it.

But accepting all of that didn't stop her from dreading the moment. So it was easier to be silent than risk letting it all spill out.

Only, the silence was also causing the kind of tension in the small confines of the car that was obviously beginning to get to him, going by the frequent, tight glances he kept flicking at her.

'What do you think it is I am taking you to?' he exploded as if on cue at her last thought. 'Hell and damnation?'

Turning her face to the car's side window, she refused to answer, and he began muttering some really choice curses, most of them in rich Italian, which quite colourfully described his irritation with sulky females, the heavy traffic on British motorways, and the whole situation in general.

'Have you always had such a filthy temper?' she asked coldly when he eventually sizzled into silence.

'No, I caught it from you,' he replied, changing lanes and increasing his speed, mainly, she suspected, because it gave him something to do. 'With anyone else I am as cool-tempered as an arctic frost.'

'That surprises me.'

'Why should it?' he threw back. 'I run a multinational corporation. You don't do that efficiently when you let your emotions rule your head.'

'The Italian temperament is notoriously volatile,' was all she said to that.

It was like a red rag being waved at an angry bull. 'I make love in Italian too,' he gritted, drawing a parallel even he didn't understand.

'Your first name is French, though, isn't it?'

He nodded. 'My mother was French,' he explained. 'My father Italian. But I was born and bred in the city of Philadelphia. The Mongrel, you used to like to call me,' he added with a smile. 'So I used to retaliate and call you—'

'The Alleycat,' she said.

His foot slipped off the accelerator. She straightened in her seat and the ensuing silence was stunned.

'You remember,' he breathed, getting a hold of himself only enough to concentrate on his driving, while she continued to sit there staring straight ahead and looking pale again.

Seeing the sickly pallor, he began to get worried, 'Samantha,' he prompted, suddenly feeling trapped there on a three-lane motorway doing seventy miles an hour. 'Talk to me,' he commanded.

But it became clear that she couldn't. With a flashing glance in his mirrors, he indicated and began switching lanes. If the worst came to the worst, he decided, he could pull onto the hard shoulder now, without causing a multi-car pile-up.

His jaw felt like a piece of rock. Reaching across the central console, he took a tight hold on her hands where she held them knotted together on her lap. 'Speak,' he ordered tightly.

This time he managed to get through to her. 'I'm all right,' she insisted, but they both knew that she wasn't. 'I'm not going to fall into a hysterical fit.'

'Ask me the same question,' he mocked. Then he saw a sign up ahead warning of a service exit and threw up a silent thanks to whoever had put it there.

A few minutes later he was pulling them into a parking bay, shutting down the engine, then climbing out of the car and swinging around the long bonnet to open her door. She was still too pale, too still.

'Come on,' he said, firmly urging her out of the car and into his arms. The worst of it was that she went without a murmur, burying her face into his throat then just standing there, letting his warmth and his strength infuse a little bit of both back into her.

'Sorry,' she murmured eventually, straightening away from him a little. 'It was shock, that's all, to hear myself saying it and know I was speaking the truth.'

His hands came up to cup her face, lifting it so he could search her clouded eyes. 'It was no big thing,' he gently dismissed. 'I suppose we should be worrying if you *don't* have the occasional memory flash.'

'Is that what the doctor said?'

'Yes,' he confirmed. 'But I'm not supposed to push it, which I did just now by bringing up the past. So it's me who should be apologising, not you.'

It was such a sweet thing to say she wanted to start crying. Maybe he saw the tears threatening, because his tone suddenly became very brisk. 'Now we've stopped, let's go and find a drink and a sandwich or something.'

Subject over—put away. Samantha had no wish to argue with that decision.

Half an hour later they were back on the road, and the day was beginning to draw in around them. After a coffee and a sandwich she was feeling a bit better, less tense about the whole London situation, and definitely more relaxed with him. 'Tell me about Bressingham,' she said.

He glanced at her, then away again, and for a while she thought he wasn't going to answer. It was, after all, another part of that past he had made taboo between them. 'You remember something else?' he questioned eventually.

'Just the name.'

He nodded, and took another few moments to take this reply in. 'The Bressingham is a hotel,' he then announced. That was all, no elaboration.

Samantha began to frown. 'One of yours?' she asked.

'We occupy six major sites in London alone,' he supplied.

'Is that where I met you? Did I work at the Bressingham Hotel?'

'Yes,' he said.

'Which is why Stefan Reece specifically connected the hotel with me,' she therefore concluded.

'Just look at that,' he suddenly exclaimed, indicating the road directly ahead of them. 'We are about to be engulfed in one hell of a cloudburst, looking at the spray coming off the road.'

He was right and they were. It hit almost at the same moment they noticed it. 'No talking now, while I concentrate,' André instructed as the windscreen wipers leapt into life.

Sublimely unaware that she had been smoothly put through several diversions in the last sixty seconds, Samantha didn't even think of arguing when they were shrouded in a wet grey mist which cut visibility down to an absolute minimum.

To ease the silence, he reached out and switched on the radio, and two seconds later a preset pop station began singing out the latest rock ballad obsessing the pop charts at the moment.

He didn't bother to change the station and she didn't mind the music. So they drove on through the rain cocooned in their own small, dry world with the music and inane DJ chatter to keep them company, and the steady swish of the car wiper-blades slowly luring Samantha into a light slumber.

From the corner of his eye André saw her body relax and was at last able to ease some of the tension out of his own. There was a very fine line between telling outright lies and merely bending the truth a little, he observed very grimly. Reflecting on their last conversation, he couldn't quite clear it with his conscience that he had managed to tread that fine line all the way.

The problem was that the Bressingham was one of several major issues that had placed them in this situation in the first place. And, until he had decided which issue to tackle first, he had no wish to tackle any.

'Ever heard the adage that real life is stranger than

fiction?' The DJ's voice cut into his brooding. 'Well, listen to this...'

Go to hell, André thought, and switched stations. He had his own stranger-than-real-life situation tying him in knots right here. He didn't need to listen to anyone else's!

The rain stopped as they were driving down the Kensington Road. As if sensing the difference when the wipers fell silent, Samantha stirred, stretched, opened her eyes, and found herself staring straight into a pair of warmly familiar dark brown eyes.

'Hi,' he murmured softly, and her stomach turned over.

'Hi,' she responded, feeling shy beneath the intimacy of his gaze. Stupid she knew, after the kind of intimacies they'd shared this afternoon. But she still made quite a play out of sitting up properly to give her an excuse to break that eye contact.

'Where are we?' she asked, glancing out of the window.

'Stuck in traffic,' he answered wryly. 'You slept for over an hour,' he added as the car began crawling forward. 'Which had me wondering if you didn't sleep much last night.'

Last night felt a long way away to Samantha—several very long lifetimes in fact. 'The rain's stopped,' she said. It was her way of ignoring his question.

'Only just,' he replied, and turned off at the next junction, taking them past place names she recognised but didn't know why she did. If anyone had asked her she would have claimed never to have even visited London, never mind lived here.

'You have a house and—what did you say—six hotels in London?' she remarked. 'Wouldn't it be easier to simply occupy one of your own suites than take on the added expense of a house?'

'Oh, very prudent-thinking.' He grinned.

The grin sent her stomach flipping again, but the words didn't, because she was very aware that prudence had been her closest companion during the last tough year.

'Living in hotels all the time is like living on top of the job,' he explained. 'Hotels are fine if we only need to be somewhere for a couple of days. But in the long term we both prefer our own private living space.'

And Samantha didn't miss the smooth way he was including her into what he was saying.

'So we have an apartment in New York, where my head office is situated,' he went on. 'Another in Paris and one in Milan. And a villa in the Caribbean for when we feel the need to really get right away and crash out on a beach for a while.'

'Lotus-eaters?' she likened dryly.

'When the mood take us,' he agreed. 'But, as for the rest of the time, we work hard, travel far, and live out of suitcases.'

'In luxury penthouse suites, like the one in Exeter,' she provided.

'Perks of the job,' he said.

'Extravagant perks of the job.'

'Great lifestyle, though. You love it,' he added as a lazy tease.

'Me?' she turned to stare at him, not sure she liked the sound of the pampered, jet-setting person he was making her out to be.

The car slowed and made an abrupt right turn. Looking ahead of them again, she only had time to register a wide expanse of black wrought-iron railings flanked by a thick green neatly clipped hedge. Then they were coming to a stop in front of a pair of tall wrought-iron gates. Beyond the gates stood a house, a beautiful white rendered house that looked like a small Georgian mansion set in its own private grounds.

The gates began to open automatically. Tyres crunched on gravel as they drove through, then began passing between two beautifully kept lawns with neatly laid borders. He drew them to a stop directly in front of a shallow porch supported by two slender round pillars, either side of which stood two great stone urns, spilling with a shock of flame-red geraniums.

Opening her door, Samantha climbed out, then just stood there staring. In the grey and muggy half-light of a cloud-cast and damp summer evening it all looked very white, very pristine, very elegant, yet…

I don't like this place, she thought suddenly. And went so icy cold that she shivered.

From the other side of the car, André was grimly observing her response, so he saw the stillness followed by the telling little shiver, knew exactly why it had happened and wondered tautly if she did.

Tension pulled like a vice across his shoulders while he waited for her to say something. He needed her to give him a clue as to what was happening so he could then decide how to respond. The house could be the key to unlock the holocaust. Certainly, there was good reason for it to do so.

But then, he had believed that seeing him for the first time would have done it, but it hadn't.

Neither had the mention of the Bressingham.

'You and I actually *live* here?' she questioned unsteadily.

The vice gave way. He relaxed his shoulders. 'Yes,'

he confirmed, amazed that his voice could sound so steady when really he was shaking with relief.

'I'll get the luggage later,' he said and, without looking at her, he walked around the car and beneath the porch with his key at the ready. 'Are you coming?' he prompted lightly.

No, Samantha answered silently, not understanding why this house was having such a powerful, muscle-dragging effect on her. But the feeling was too strong for her to ignore it. So she remained where she was, clinging to the open door of the Jaguar, watching him place the key in the door, then send it swinging open.

Her breath caught in her throat and congealed there in a thick, suffocating ball. He too, had gone very still— no movement, no sign of anything. As if, like herself, he was waiting for something monumental to happen. Silence thumped and throbbed in the warm, muggy atmosphere, the complete stillness all aiding and abetting that silence to wrap tight pressure bands around her chest, until a roaring began to build inside her head.

No, she willed herself hazily. I won't faint away again—I won't!

Maybe he sensed her silent battle because he turned suddenly to face her. Big, lean and so devastatingly attractive. She felt sick with how strong her feelings were for him. It hurt, it actually hurt like a physical pain, because she just could not bring herself to believe that he felt the same for her.

'Tell me why you married me,' she whispered, having to squeeze the words past the ball in her throat.

His face seemed carved from stone. 'Why does any man marry a beautiful woman?' he countered levelly.

The 'beautiful' did not come into the equation. She didn't even want to hear it there. It changed the emphasis too much. Made the beauty more important than the woman.

Yet... She dropped her eyes from his and began to frown at the ground in blind confusion, because 'beauty' didn't seem to be her problem here. It was something else that was bothering her, gnawing at her, warning her. But what else? What—what else...?

'If I could marry you again tomorrow, I would do so.' A crunch of gravel and she looked up to find him walking towards her, the dark solemnity of his expression a hypnotic balm. 'If you ran away again I would look for you until the day I die.'

'But you didn't search the first time,' she whispered hoarsely, feeling as if she was trapped on a never-ending treadmill with that single question being the chain that held her there.

He smiled, if you could call it a smile. A twist of derision? Of mockery? Of grim, dark irony?

Then, with a lightning movement of lean, lithe muscle, he suddenly grabbed hold of the Jaguar door and the car bonnet on the other side of her, trapping her with his body, his strength—and with his anger. She gasped. His teeth glinted white between his stretched lips. And his eyes flashed like black diamonds, as hard as hell.

'It wasn't me who lost you, *mia cara*,' he incised very thinly. 'It was you that lost yourself.'

Sparks crackled in the air between them. Electric impulses began flashing in her brain. Doors opened, then slammed shut before she could so much as glimpse what was going on behind them. Her heart began to race. Her breasts lifted and fell in a hectic, shallow attempt at breathing.

She opened her mouth, tried to speak, found that she

couldn't because those angry eyes were forcing her to acknowledge what he'd said just now.

He was right—he was right! Her panic-ridden mind began screaming at her. Like some terrible coward she had run away and lost herself rather than face whatever it was she was scared of.

How pathetic, she thought scathingly, looking hard into those ruthless eyes that were making her face her own wretched cowardice. And willed—*willed* her mind to stop playing stupid games on her so she could solve the conundrum that made this man feel like her very soul mate and her worst enemy at the same time!

'I love you, don't I?' she heard herself say in a cracked little whisper.

The eyes went absolutely black. 'Yes,' he confirmed.

'And I hurt you badly. You implied that to me once.'

He didn't like that claim, it had the eyes flicking away from her on a flash of irritation before they came back to her face again.

'For a short while,' he confirmed very grimly. 'But if you are now thinking that I brought you here to exact retribution, then don't,' he declared. 'Because I hurt you a whole lot more than you even attempted to hurt me.'

Which implied that their marriage had not been all delight and happiness, she concluded. But then, they'd already settled that point in several ways during the last couple of days.

Both hot-tempered, both passionately volatile, both stubbornly determined to have their own way.

Glancing over his shoulder, she looked at the house again. It no longer filled her with frightened dismay— though she still didn't understand why it had done in the first place.

'I still don't remember,' she said, looking back at him. 'But I want to.'

Something stirred on those rock-solid features—a slackening of tension. 'Good.' He nodded, and straightened away from her. 'Then we are beginning to make some progress at last. How is the knee? Can you use it yet?'

Diversion tactics, she noted as she glanced down to find the right knee bent, so her weight was all on the other leg. Instinctive protection, she recognised dully, no matter how big the trauma, she could still protect the wretched knee.

Neither said anything more while she went through her usual exercises to loosen the stiffness out of the joint. Then, as if by tacit agreement, the moment her foot went on the ground she reached for his arm, at the same instant that he offered it to her. Slender fingers looped round cool buff cambric then curled into solid strength. Her senses leapt, then steadied. He waited to make sure that she was ready, then turned them both towards the house.

Home, he'd called it. Her home. *Their* home. 'It's looks a bit big for just two of us,' she remarked.

'It's a— It's been in the family for a long time.'

Something in the way he hesitated then changed what he had been going to say made her stop and look up at him. But all she saw was the silken curve of dark eyelashes covering his expressive eyes. Beginning to look away from him again, she caught a glimpse of his mouth as it moved, suddenly hardening into the kind of sneer that made her fingernails dig into his arm in puzzled alarm.

The action sent his eyelashes flicking up to reveal his eyes again. Something hot was burning there, something

hard and so angry she drew in a sharp breath and tried
to step right back.

The burn became a flash, followed by a full explosion.
'Oh, to *hell* with this!' he hissed, and bent and lifted her
into his arms.

'What are you doing?' she cried out, feeling her heart
jump to her throat as hard-packed muscle met with her
shock-quivering frame. 'I'm not an invalid! I don't *need*
carrying!'

'You are my *wife*,' he gritted back. 'I don't *need* an
excuse to do *anything* with you!'

'My agreement would be nice!' she snapped right
back as he strode angrily towards the house.

He stopped on the threshold, bent his head and kissed
her with such untamed passion it was as if he actually
meant to turn her bones to dust.

By the time he lifted his head again he knew he had
succeeded. 'Yes,' he hissed. 'You might not know *who*
you are but you will know *what* you are before this day
is through,' he vowed.

'What's the matter with you?' she cried. 'Why are you
so suddenly angry?'

'*Wife!*' he snarled as if that answered everything. 'My
wife! *Ma femme a moi!*' he rasped in French. '*La mia
moglie!*' he declared in a harsh Italian—staking his claim
on all fronts like an impassioned new groom who was
carrying his virgin bride to her fate.

Only she was no new bride, and nor was she a virgin,
as they'd already well and truly substantiated once already today. Nor did whatever his intentions were
frighten her in the slightest. If anything, she felt terribly
exhilarated.

The door slammed shut behind them, and she gained
a vague impression of a classical Georgian interior:

pastel silk walls; elegant cornices; oil paintings that must have cost the earth but went by in a blur as he kept on walking down a rectangular hall towards the stairwell.

'André—'

'Shut up,' he cut in, chin jutted and locked in grim determination. 'Don't so much as dare say my name until I've got you safely horizontal.'

'Why?' she asked curiously.

'Because you usually avoid saying it. In fact, you only say it when you don't realise you're saying it. It makes me wild,' he gritted. 'Makes me feel as though I only take physical form in the realms of your imagination.'

He began mounting the stairs while Samantha absorbed what he'd said and realised he'd said it perfectly. Touch him and she knew him. Stand apart and he became a shadowy figment she could never quite see in full, physical shape.

'Sorry,' she whispered, and touched an apologetic kiss to the rigid line of his jaw a kiss that immediately became something else entirely.

A bite, an open-mouthed, fully fledged, salacious bite, that sank its teeth into warm and living skin on bone and would have drawn blood—only that was not the objective. The objective was to flick a tongue over rasping skin in need of shaving and taste the man—taste him. It was compulsive. A desire that arrived from nowhere and completely took her over.

His shoulders flexed, his skin grew hot, and the air left his throat on a hoarse scrape. 'Witch,' he gritted. But he liked it. She could feel the pleasure rippling through him as another door opened and closed. Then he was leaning heavily back against it, and with a jerk he freed his jaw and paid her back by claiming her mouth with a kiss that was hot and deep and so hungry it wanted to devour.

Samantha was quite happy to be devoured. It was that elemental.

Even when he allowed her feet to slide to the floor, that kiss wasn't broken. This was need, hot and fevered. This was sex at its most animal. He grabbed the edge of her top and raked it up her body and over her head. She lifted her arms up to aid its departure, groaning in anguish when their mouths had to part to allow the top to pass between them.

He removed his own shirt with no help from her; she was too busy touching his hair, touching his face with hungry fingers. And after that she became lost in a world of male textures. Satin-smooth shoulders, springy black chest hair—tight male nipples that she took greedily into her mouth.

His breathing had gone haywire, chest rising and sinking in rapid rhythm with his heartbeat. And where his fingers slid in the most excruciatingly light caresses she became a live conduit to pure sexual pleasure. Her bra sprang free. With a boneless fluidity that defied the fact that she was standing on her own two feet, she stepped back and flicked the bra away, then stood, chin up, eyes like emerald fires, proudly offering him the chance to taste.

On a growl, he came away from the door. 'You haven't forgotten this, have you?' he gritted. 'You still remember how to seduce me out of my skin!'

She touched that skin. One long and slender arm made another fluid movement and her fingers were resting against a hair-free, satin, taut pectoral.

Hard muscle flexed beneath her fingers. She sent him a provoking smile.

It was a smile that made him lose touch with the last dregs of reason. 'You're not of this world,' he muttered rawly, wrapped his arms around her and lifted her back off her feet.

'Neither are you,' she replied. Then, 'André,' she murmured tauntingly into his hard, dark, handsome face. 'Are you real or aren't you?'

'You're about to find out,' he said, dropping her down onto a high, French-style antique bed; he pushed her to lie back, then with a few grimly economical movements began unfastening his trousers. Her shoes fell off, a set of bare toes came up to rub against the centre of his chest, and his eyes narrowed into glinting slits which threatened retribution as he stood over her and let her torment him while he rid himself of his clothes.

She didn't know that this was the real Samantha playing her old sensual games, André mused grimly. If she did know she would not be seducing him, but screaming at him like a maniac.

But instinct had taken over. And instinct was instinct, whether or not it had the memories to go along with it. And the real Samantha's instinct was to tease and to provoke and to play the seductress until she drove her poor victim crazy.

What lack of memory didn't tell her was that this poor victim had taken her measure a long time ago. Anything she could dish out he could give back tenfold. It was one of the major ingredients that had made their marriage so excitingly volatile. But, as with any volatile substance, it was also dangerously unpredictable. And it was just that unpredictability which had finally torn them both to shreds in the end—because neither had been able to trust the other not to behave like this with anyone else.

Mistrust led to suspicion, and suspicion to lies. When he'd first met her she'd had no less than three boyfriends in tow. Three other men knowing her like this? Three other lovers to share the addiction? The very idea had driven him into taking some desperate measures to gain exclusive rights to this beautiful, wanton, glorious woman.

Within the month he had married her, holding the arrogant belief that marriage was all it would take to tame the tiger that lived inside her. What he'd actually discovered was that he had his own tiger, waiting to leap out and roar. Despite discovering Samantha was a virgin, her tiger became an intense sexual appetite. His tiger was jealousy. He'd had to lose her to discover that her seductress act had hidden a vulnerable heart, which had only wanted him to love her but could not quite believe that he did.

Jealousy was love's natural predator. It was mean and cruel and naturally devious. So he'd fed her desire and had held back that which she had needed most from him—his love. In the end it had killed her—or as good as, when he saw what it had left her with. This… The desire for his body. And a fear so great, of the love resurrecting itself, that she preferred to remember nothing than risk going through that torment again.

So, what did all of that say about him? he finally concluded. Standing here in front of her—bold in his nakedness, with her foot circling exquisitely arousing caresses against his flesh as he prepared to begin feeding those desires again.

'André?' she murmured questioningly, because he'd been standing there too long doing nothing but stare at her.

André. Dear God, the name ripped him to pieces with self-contempt, disgust and a sickening dismay.

'No,' he uttered thickly, stepping back from the foot then turning his back on her so he didn't have to watch while she shattered.

She didn't say a word, not one word. Her silence cut into him like a nine-inch steel blade.

'We won't do this again unless we do so as equals,' he told her flatly.

'Equals?' he heard her whisper.

'Yes!' he barked, dragging up the zip over a burgeoning shaft which was making an absolute mockery out of his grand gesture. He swung round to sear her with the flame of his own filthy anger. 'Equals as in you saying my name and *knowing* this man called *André* who you are about to give your body to!' he all but snarled at her.

She was sitting up, hair a mass of crackling fire around her shoulders and coiling sensually over her lily-white breasts. But her face was whiter, and he saw her flinch, saw her beautiful eyes fill with the horrible glint of shame. Remorse almost choked him. He'd started this. He'd given in to temptation when he'd promised himself he wouldn't, done it all on the flimsy excuse to himself that he was diverting her attention away from what they had been discussing.

'I do know him,' she said quietly. 'He's a rat.'

She was right and he was. His anger melted down into grim self-mockery. 'Well, the rat is going to go scavenging in the kitchen,' he threw back satirically. 'Get dressed and come and join me when you're ready.'

With that he got out of there before she threw something lethal at him. Instincts were instincts after all, and Samantha's instincts were all damned dangerous...

CHAPTER TEN

SHE didn't go down. He had to be crazy to think that she actually would.

Or just plain arrogant.

What she did was remain sitting on the edge of the bed, silently drowning in a pool of her own humiliation. And it was all her own. Because she'd done it all by her stupid self. He might have started it but she'd certainly encouraged it. When she should have been pushing him away she'd kissed him, bitten him, lured him and provoked him like a sex-mad teenager without a moral in sight.

Sex-mad. She shivered, feeling goose-bumps of dismay break out all over her flesh. At least they had a strong enough effect to make her get up and gather up her clothes with the intention of putting them back on. Then she just stood there, looking around the bedroom with its beautiful French furniture as if none of it was even there. Then, without thinking twice about it, she dropped the clothes to the floor again, walked back to the bed and crawled beneath the cool white percale duvet, shut her eyes and sank into a deep, dark slumber filled with dancing nymphets and leering dark devils.

She awoke hours later, feeling heavy-eyed and so sluggish she could almost believe she had drunk herself into a bad hangover.

That would be a first, she thought with a smile, and got out of the bed to walk into the bathroom, where she showered, dried herself, strolled across the thick creamy carpet towards another door that led into the dressing room. Taking her time, she selected a long, emerald-green, Japanese silk robe, slipped it on and began tying the silk belt around her waist as she walked back into the bedroom. Her head was down, watching her busy fingers, and her movements were as smooth and relaxed as anyone's should be who was moving around their own bedroom, in their own home.

André was away, she was thinking idly. Raoul was out on the town somewhere. Which meant she had the whole house to herself to—

That was when she noticed the suitcase standing by the door, frowned at it—then heard a sound across the room and turned her head to see André, dressed in black silk trousers and a white silk shirt, standing by the window, with his hands in his pockets and his handsome face wearing a very sternly closed expression.

'You found your old clothes, then,' he said, and—slam. A door flew shut in her head and she sank onto the soft cream carpet.

The next thing she knew she was lying on a strange bed, wearing a beautiful green silk wrap she didn't recognise, and a complete stranger was leaning over her.

Youngish, good-looking. 'Hi.' He smiled pleasantly when he saw she was looking at him. 'Beautiful eyes. I'm glad you opened them.'

'Where am I?' she mumbled hazily. 'Who are you?'

'I'm a doctor.' He smiled again. 'The name is Jonathan Miles, though people I really like are allowed to call me Jack.'

It was only then that she realised he was lightly clasping one of her wrists, where the pulse was throbbing dully beneath his fingers.

'Now, stay still for a moment while I get close and intimate by looking deep into those beautiful eyes with this torch...'

Obediently she did as instructed. 'What happened?' she asked as he began flashing the torch into one of her eyes.

'You blacked out,' he explained, moving onto the other eye. 'André was worried, so he called me in to check you over.'

André. At last the mist clouding her brain began to clear.

'Do you know where you are?' he asked her quietly.

'Yes,' she mumbled.

'Can you tell me the last thing you remember before you blacked out?'

'I woke up. I knew who I was. Realised it and blacked out,' she replied with quiet economy.

He began to frown. 'What made you realise?'

Him, she wanted to spit. I hate him. I don't ever want to set eyes on him again. And, acting on that thought, she let her eyes drift shut again. 'I prefer not to talk about it,' she said.

The doctor sat back with a dissatisfied sigh. 'Too upsetting or too—private?' he quizzed.

Both, she thought and refused to answer. The silence dragged. Somewhere else in the room a body shifted tensely. The doctor's fingers lightly touched the fine scar at her temple. Her eyes flicked back open, hard green, sparking with warning.

'Nice job.' He smiled that pleasant smile again. 'A superficial laceration that should disappear completely given time,' he said in diagnosis. 'What about the knee?'

'The knee is fine,' she answered tightly. 'Like everything that's wrong with me, it just needs time.'

The doctor studied her angry, pale, defensive face for a few moments, then nodded. 'Point taken,' he conceded. 'Bearing that in mind, I suppose you won't agree to a head X-ray, just to check that there is nothing—'

'No,' she interrupted firmly.

'Yes,' another voice chipped in. 'If you feel its necessary, Jack, then she'll do it.'

The moment André made his presence truly felt, Samantha covered her eyes with a hand.

'This isn't your decision, André,' she heard the doctor say with a flat-voiced firmness that quietly impressed her. And if she'd been watching she would have seen him flash a warning look at the other man, which had him swinging away in grim frustration.

She would have also seen the doctor pick up her two packs of tablets from the bedside cabinet where, unbeknown to her, André had fished them out of her handbag and placed them. Jack Miles read the two pharmacy labels, grimaced, then opened one and flipped out a small white pill before deftly pocketing the rest and reaching for a glass of water.

'Here, take this,' he instructed.

The hand slid away. She frowned at the pill, recognised it and obediently took it from him, drank it down with the water then closed her eyes to wait for the mild tranquilliser to soothe away everything.

She felt the bed shift as the doctor stood up, then his hand gently resting on one of hers for a moment. 'André knows where I am if you need me, Samantha.'

'Mmm,' she said. 'Thanks.' And was just glad he was going.

The moment Jack gave him the nod, André strode for the door and the two men left quietly. He felt like hell, and by the expression on Jack's face he felt that André deserved it.

'I don't know what game you think you're playing here, André…' Jack Miles went on the attack as soon as the door closed behind him '…but I'm going to tell you that it's a dangerous one.'

'It isn't a game,' he threw back grimly.

'I'm glad you realise that,' the doctor said. 'But if you brought me here for my honest opinion, then I think you're in over your head. Amnesia is a tricky condition. We know very little about it. But I would say that she is beginning to remember. And, personally, I think she needs a controlled environment in which to do so.'

'No,' André refused instantly, and turned to walk towards the stairwell. 'You're talking hospitals, and though I might see the sense in her having a quick X-ray, I will *not* put her back into hospital. She's had enough of those to last her a lifetime,' he added with a tense shift of his shoulders.

'Which doesn't necessarily make you her best alternative.'

'I'm her *only* alternative!' he barked, swinging round to glare at the other man. 'She relates to me! She responds to me! She needs me to be here for her and I won't let her down again!'

It was possessive and it was passionate. Jack studied his tight, determined features, and grimaced. 'Your own personal crusade, André?' he suggested.

'Yes,' André hissed, and turned away again to stride down the stairs, wanting Jack to go now, since he wasn't telling him anything he didn't know already. In over his head? Hell, he knew it. Stick her in a controlled environment? Not while he still had breath left in his body to stop it from happening.

'Here...' At the front door, Jack fished the two packs of tablets out of his pocket and handed them to him. 'You keep these away from her,' he advised. 'Administer only when *you* believe they are necessary.'

'You mean—' His mouth went dry. 'You think she's...'

'I think she's in shock, damn it!' The other man suddenly exploded. 'When did you find her? Two days ago? How many times did you say she'd blacked out or almost blacked out since then? Who knows what's happening inside her head? I certainly don't. You obviously don't. And I don't think that she knows either! Tonight, for instance,' he continued furiously, 'she goes to sleep, wakes up—and starts using that bedroom as if she'd never spent a year away from it! Then all of a sudden, wham, she somersaults back from the past into the present—it's no wonder she blacks out!'

'I get the picture,' André said roughly, grimly pocketing the tablets and wanting to shut him up so that he would just go. 'Thanks for coming out at such short notice, Jack. It was appreciated.'

'But not the opinion, hmm?' Jack Miles noted dryly. 'Well, just one last piece of advice before I leave,' he went on. 'If you feel you must deal with this problem yourself, then take it easy. Give her comfort, support and just be there for her. But no probing,' he warned with deadly seriousness. 'And maybe, just maybe, you'll get lucky and the memories will simply float gently to the surface and emerge without causing her further trauma.'

'But you don't think it will be that easy.' André grimaced, reading the doubtful tone in his voice.

Jack shook his head. 'As she's proved already, things are coming back in disjointed flashes. And you are the trigger, André. Don't, for goodness' sake, squeeze that trigger, or the gun might backfire in your face.'

It backfired twelve months ago, André thought heavily as he closed the door on Jack Miles's departure. Sighing, he turned and walked into the sitting room, then aimed directly for the whisky decanter. As he poured the drink, his eyes caught sight of a framed photograph sitting on the top of the antique bureau which was the only piece of furniture Samantha had brought with her into the house when they'd married.

Stepping over to it, he picked up the photo frame and stood staring down at the faces of two laughing young men. Then, with a violence that erupted out of nowhere, he threw the frame to the floor, smashing it to smithereens.

The next morning Samantha came down the stairs and turned towards the back of the house, following the aroma of toast and freshly ground coffee. In truth, her stomach was beginning to think her throat had been cut, it was so long since she'd swallowed anything more substantial that a pre-packed sandwich at a motorway café.

But it still took courage to open the door she presumed led into the kitchen, not at all sure who she was going see on the other side of it. Stranger or half-stranger?

Half-stranger, she discovered. A very dark, very attractive one, wearing a v-necked sweatshirt and a pair of stone-washed trousers. He was standing in front of a very impressive stainless steel cooking range, feeding slices of bread into a rotating grill. Glancing round, he saw her standing in the doorway, and a short tense stillness followed in which she gazed warily at him and he stared warily back.

Stalemate. Neither knew what to say to the other. Neither knew how the other was going to react. He broke the deadlock first by dipping his eyes over the simple corn-yellow blouse she had teamed with a pair of pale olive trousers and a matching gilet. And if he recognised them as items from the wardrobe upstairs, this time he had the caution to say nothing, and with a smooth-spoken, 'Hi,' he turned his attention back to what he was doing. 'Did the smell of the coffee get as far as your room?'

'The toast, actually,' she replied, striving to sound as relaxed as he did. 'I'm starving,' she admitted.

'I know the feeling. I didn't eat much myself yester-day. Sit down,' he invited. 'Sustenance will arrive in about ten seconds.'

Well, that was the most awkward part over, she mused as she did as she was told and went to sit down at the large, scrubbed kitchen table that dominated the room. Then, to stop herself from looking at him, she made herself take an interest in her surroundings.

The kitchen was gorgeous, packed full of individually standing, old, scrubbed pine furniture you would only expect to find in a traditional farmhouse. 'Who did the interior decorating for you?' she questioned curiously.

'My mother,' he replied, deftly stacking hot slices of toast onto a hot plate. 'Hence the French influence in just about everything you see.

His mother. Her heart sank. 'Does she live here as well?' she asked, silently pleading for him to say no.

He went many steps further than her plea with a quiet, 'She died several years ago.'

Which made her feel really mean for what she had been thinking. 'I'm sorry,' she murmured.

He just offered a shrug as he turned to put the plate

of toast down on the table, followed by a big old-fashioned coffee pot. 'The two of you never met,' he told her, and turned away again.

'Your father?' She felt compelled to ask next.

Two serviceable white coffee mugs and a couple of white side plates arrived on the table along with milk, sugar and butter dish. 'He died when I was ten years old.'

'Oh, I'm sorry,' she said again, then clamped her mouth shut. And because they were both aware that it was a natural progression for her to go on and ask if there were any other members of his family, a very loud silence fell.

But she couldn't ask—though she didn't understand *why* she couldn't.

In an attempt to fill the gap, she reached for the coffee mugs, carefully lining them up in front of her while she racked her brains for something else to say. 'I would have expected a house the size of this to have a small army of servants to keep it so nice,' she remarked.

'They come in on a daily basis during week days,' he explained, pulling out the chair opposite hers and sitting down. 'Today is Saturday,' he added, for no reason that Samantha could see other than to keep the conversation moving.

'Should I know any of them?' she asked, picking up the coffee pot.

'Mrs Saunders, who keeps the house, you knew. As to the rest, I have no idea.'

'Oh,' was all she could find to say to that. So she turned her attention to pouring coffee into both of the mugs, adding sugar to one and milk to the other, then she slid the sugared black one across the table towards him.

'Thanks,' he murmured a trifle thickly.

She nodded in acknowledgement, took a sip at her coffee, selected a slice of toast, placed it on one of the white side plates, then just sat there blankly staring at it.

'What?' he said gruffly. 'Something wrong? Something I—'

'Knife,' she explained.

It was his turn to look blank as he stared at the table for a few seconds before he got up and went to a drawer, coming back with several knives which he placed down on the table.

'You've hurt your finger,' she observed, noticing the heavy plaster wrapping encasing the index finger on his right hand.

'I dropped a glass,' he lied, 'and cut myself when I was picking up the broken pieces. While I'm up, do you want marmalade or jam?'

Samantha shook her head and he sat down again. Picking up her coffee, she sipped at it for a while. He did the same. When she buttered her slice of toast so did he. It was awful, she decided glumly. Neither of them had a single thing worth saying. Strangers did not even cover what they were to each other any more.

'Did you—?'

'Have you—?'

Both began speaking at once, and both stopped at once.

'You go first,' he invited.

Great, Samantha thought! She'd forgotten what she had been going to say.

Story of my life, she mocked. 'I think I'll have that jam.' She plucked the words out of thin air.

He got up. Her temper began to fray under the stress. 'I didn't expect you to get it for me,' she snapped. 'All you needed to do was point me in the right direction and I would have managed to find it myself!'

The jam pot landed with a thud on the table. 'No problem,' he clipped.

Lying swine, she thought, and came to her feet. He was still standing. 'Where are you going now?' He sighed the words out impatiently.

'It's you who's been jumping up and down,' she threw back.

'Just—sit and eat,' he commanded. Not looking so smooth around his own sleek edges now, she noticed waspishly.

'I'm not hungry—'

'Sit down and *eat*!' he repeated angrily.

'I can't!' she cried. 'I feel as if you've got me pinned under a microscope!'

His sigh seemed to rake over ever inch of him. 'Okay,' he said. 'Point taken. I'll eat later. But for goodness' sake,' he added angrily, 'eat something, Samantha... Eat!'

With that he strode out of the kitchen, making her feel miserable and guilty for driving him away. So she ate— force-fed herself, in fact. She drank some coffee, then got up and made fresh of both coffee and toast, placed them on a tray and, on a deep breath for courage, went looking for him.

He was easier to find than she'd expected. She simply followed the muffled sound of his angry voice and found him sitting behind a desk in a beautiful study, lined wall-to-wall with brass-grilled bookcases which looked as old as the house.

He was talking on the phone, but the moment he saw her come through the door he broke the conversation and returned the receiver to its rest.

'Peace offering.' She smiled nervously, carrying the loaded tray over to the desk and setting it down. 'I'm sorry I caused all of that…strife, in the kitchen.'

'My fault,' he said instantly.

'No it wasn't.' She refused to let him be that gracious. 'It was mine. I was nervous—still am as a matter of fact,' she admitted

'Pour the coffee,' he instructed.

Grimacing at the way he had coolly passed over her carefully planned apology, she did as he bade and poured the coffee, then silently handed it to him. She received no thanks, only a glinting look in those wretched eyes that could have held amusement as he took the coffee mug from her.

'You're a hard man, Signor Visconte,' she informed him dryly, and turned to leave.

'And you, Signora Visconte,' he returned, 'are the most amazingly unpredictable woman I know.'

'Compliment or censure?' She mused out loud.

He laughed. 'Oh, most definitely a compliment,' he assured. 'No—don't go,' he added when she made to do just that, and the husky warmth of his voice vibrated on her senses, bringing her to a very wary standstill.

What now? she wondered, already beginning to pull up her defences again—just in case.

'Give me two minutes to consume your…peace offering and I'll reacquaint you with the house, if you like…'

Her defences fell again, that tentative 'if you like' helping to tumble them. She nodded her agreement. The telephone rang. It helped ease them through the next, few, awkward seconds. He answered it; she wandered off to peer inside the brass grilles at the selection of priceless first-edition books she could see locked safely out of reach.

'Has anyone bothered reading them?' she asked when the phone went down again.

'Not in my lifetime,' he drawled. 'They belonged to my grandfather on my Italian side. This house belonged to *his* English mother. The melting pot of culture swimming in my blood is astonishing when you think about it,' he mocked.

The true mongrel, Samantha thought, and smiled to herself because that blood had to be a rare mix of very old money when you put all the evidence together.

'They should be in a museum,' Samantha remarked.

'The books or my family?'

'The books.' She laughed, swinging round to toss that laugh at him.

His eyes dilated; she saw it happen as his attention riveted on this first laughing response she had offered him. Her heart-rate quickened, sending a rush of awareness surging to her head. Then, with a blink of his long lashes, he recovered, her heart-rate slowed and the awareness faded.

'The books belong to the house.' He continued with the conversation as if the stinging moment in between had never been there. 'I am only their guardian. Even my very French mother, who respected nothing if it wasn't French, didn't dare lay a finger them.'

'You say that very cynically. But she married an Italian who lived in America. Surely that says she must have loved your father very much.'

'That was her first marriage. She married her second husband the year after my father died. He was as French as she was.'

Samantha frowned. 'But I thought you said you were brought up in Philadelphia?'

'Not by her choice but my father's choice. He was the one with the money and therefore the power—even from the grave.' Suddenly the cynicism was really pronounced. 'If my mother wanted to keep her hands on the money then she had to agree to keep me, as his sole beneficiary, where that money was generated.'

'You didn't get on with her,' Samantha murmured softly.

'You are mistaken,' he said coldly. 'I adored her. She and Ra—'

He stopped quite suddenly, snapping his lips together on whatever he had been about to say. Yet another of those strained silences fell round them, making Samantha frown and André look angry.

The ring of the telephone actually startled the pair of them as it pealed out its demand. He snatched it up. 'What?' he rapped out, then sat there frowning and listening while Samantha hunted through the conversation, looking for a logical reason for the sudden silence. The books? The mother? The stepfather whose name he didn't quite finish?

'Right now, you mean?' he questioned sharply. 'Okay, that's great.' He stood up. 'No, now is fine. I'll have to change into a suit, but set it up and I'll be there.'

The phone went down.

'I have to go out,' he said to Samantha. 'I'm sorry. Would you mind showing yourself around the house?'

'Of course not,' she assured him.

'Thanks,' he murmured. 'I shouldn't be long.' He was already striding for the door. 'Feel free to make yourself at home while I'm gone.'

'I thought it *was* my home,' she whispered into the

empty space he had left behind him, and felt slightly offended by the speed with which he had made his escape—almost as if he'd been relieved by the excuse to get away from her for a while.

No, she scolded herself. The man is important. He runs a multinational business. Of course he has to keep his priorities in perspective.

And that was the second lot of toast and coffee he had walked away from this morning, she thought with a rueful smile. Sighing to herself, she picked the tray up again and carried it back to the kitchen, thinking, Now I am even beginning to feel like a wife. Unappreciated and put to one side.

'I've just thought...' His voice came at her from behind. 'You will wait here, won't you? You won't be tempted to go out, without me to—'

'Keep an eye on me?' she finished for him, turning to throw him a fiery glare.

A glare that fizzled out when she saw him standing there in a grey suit, white shirt and blue silk tie. In the space of what felt like only five minutes he had transformed himself from casual man about the house into hard-edged man of the City.

Handsome, sharp. Powerful—sexy...

'I just don't think I should be leaving you alone right now,' he explained.

Samantha frowned. 'Go to your meeting,' she told him. 'I'm not stupid. And I have no intention of doing anything stupid.'

'And that,' he drawled sardonically, 'is most definitely my cue to get out of here before we start yet another row.'

He went to leave; her eyes began to hurt. 'Was it always like this between us?' she asked thickly.

'Yes,' he admitted. 'We fight as we make love: with no holds barred.'

His beautiful mouth moved on a grimace and Samantha grimaced herself. 'No wonder our marriage barely lasted a year, then,' she said. And, seeing his hesitation, his desire to say something in answer to her last comment, Samantha turned her back on him again, with a, 'See you later,' gauged to finish the discussion before, as he'd predicted, it developed into something else.

He clearly thought the very same thing, because he left with only a flat, 'Sure.'

It was a relief to have him gone. A relief to have time to walk through the house without feeling under the constant surveillance of a pair of dark eyes that seemingly expected everything she saw to be the magic key that opened the floodgates to her memory.

The house didn't do it. Walking from room to room, the only thing she did learn was that his mother had possessed a truly unimpeachable eye for what was the best in good taste and classical styling. One room blended smoothly with another in a flow of pastel shades and exquisite furniture pieces that must have cost the earth.

By the time she arrived back where she'd started from, Samantha had to ask herself why she had been so afraid of coming into this house yesterday. Because, on the whole, she'd found the house an absolute pleasure.

Nothing had hit her as scary, nothing vaguely sinister—if she didn't count the room upstairs, which had given her a couple of uneasy moments when she'd tried the door only to find it was locked. Or the beautiful walnut roll-top bureau in the sitting room she had caught herself gently stroking as if it was a long-lost friend.

But other than for those things she simply loved every inch of the place. A point that added to the puzzle as to why she would want to turn her back on it all as if it had never existed.

Or turn her back on the man who came with it, she then added with a faint quiver she knew was more sexual than threatening.

With a small sigh, she suddenly decided to pick up the phone and call Carla at the Tremount. She'd promised she would keep in touch, and right now she felt she needed to hear a friendly voice... A truly familiar friendly voice, she extended.

But the conversation wasn't quite as comforting as that...

CHAPTER ELEVEN

LETTING himself back into the house, André paused in the hallway to listen for signs of life. Hearing none, he began searching rooms, giving himself a few uneasy moments when he couldn't find Samantha anywhere—until he had the sense to look where he would have expected to find the old Samantha.

Sure enough, even as he strode through the door connecting the sitting room with the elegant glass-domed swimming pool, he saw her cutting through the water with the smooth, clean glide of a natural-born swimmer. She was a mermaid; she always had been. Give her time to herself and she would usually find a pool somewhere to dive into, and it filled him with a real burst of pleasure to see her truly back where she belonged like this.

His first instinct was to strip to his micro-briefs then dive in there and join her—only he was wryly aware that she probably wouldn't appreciate the gesture right now, when natural responses had to be contained to their minimum.

Presuming, of course, that the Samantha swimming in the pool was the new Samantha, he then thought frowningly. He didn't think even she knew how often she'd slipped back and forth through time. He hadn't begun to realise himself until this morning, when he'd watched her pour his coffee without needing to be prompted on how he liked it. As she'd pushed the drink towards him it had finally begun to dawn on him just what was happening to her—and had been happening from the moment he'd walked back into her life.

The journey to Exeter from the Tremount, for instance, when she'd spent the whole time talking to him as if they'd never been apart. André this, André that. It had driven him crazy at the time, hearing her say his name so comfortably while still believing he was a complete stranger. Then there were the times when they'd touched or kissed or made love, he recounted with a fine, tight, sense-twisting shudder. She'd known him then, all right, and had slipped into the old Samantha mould just as naturally as she was cutting through the water right now.

So—which one was swimming in the pool—the old or the new Samantha? he asked himself.

Hell, he didn't know. But he was not going to risk finding out the hard way, by shocking her into another blackout in the middle of a pool of deep water.

So, instead of making her aware of his presence, he turned away with the intention of leaving as silently as he had arrived... Or would have done if a rather sarcastic voice hadn't stopped him.

'Well, well.' He heard her drawl. 'If it isn't the very busy, hotshot tycoon taking time out of his busy tycoon schedule to say hello...'

His skin began to prickle, the tone alone telling him that whichever Samantha it was she was angry about something. Turning round, he saw her treading water dead centre of the pool. 'Was there something specific you meant to convey in that remark?' he enquired narrowly.

'Yes,' she replied, then slid gracefully onto her back to stroke smoothly away.

Still not certain who it was he was talking to, André

stepped to the edge of the pool. 'Then, explain,' he suggested.

'I was commenting on your very busy life,' she informed him as those long slender arms lazily propelled her through the water. 'Picking up a hotel here, picking another up there... Tell me,' she begged, the sarcasm echoing high into the glass-domed roof, 'because I'll be really interested to know, is there an actual point where you can ever envisage saying to yourself that enough is enough, I don't *need* another hotel, no matter what its money-pulling potential is?'

She was talking hotels. His flesh went cold. 'Get out of the water!' he commanded harshly.

'I beg your pardon?' She gasped, and stopped swimming to stare at him.

'You heard me.' He began striding down the length of the pool with his senses on alert and his mind gone haywire. 'I want you to swim to the side of the pool and get out! I mean it, Samantha!' he warned when she made no move to comply. 'If you don't get out of there I'm coming in to drag you out!'

And to suit threat with action he pulled off his jacket and tossed it aside.

Puzzled, more than anything, he suspected, because she could see he was so deadly serious, she swam to the other side of the pool and pulled herself out. Water streamed from her body, leaving behind it a long, slender nymph with skin like a pearl and a lilac one-piece swimsuit that revealed more that it concealed... And he still didn't know which Samantha it was that turned to glare at him across the width of the pool.

'What's the matter with you?' she demanded crossly. 'I can swim like a fish! I don't need—'

'And if you'd had another blackout while you were

in there?' he raked back. 'What good would your swimming proficiency be to you then?'

Slender hands went on slender hips. Old or new? Both would challenge him with that pose. 'You're just trying to divert my attention away from what I was talking about,' she accused him. 'Do you think I haven't noticed how you like to do that? Well, forget it this time, André, because it isn't going to work—'

André. She'd just called him André.

'So let's talk about hotels,' she went on in a voice still dripping sarcasm. 'And let's talk about sneaky tycoons who move in on people as well as hotels and take them over without—'

Hell, she knew who she was all right. 'I did *not* move in on the Bressingham!' He angrily denied the charge. 'And I did *not* move in on your father! In fact it was the other way round, if you'd only...'

Something changed inside her. Samantha felt it happen. A sudden icy confusion that made her feel very peculiar as she tried to make sense of a misunderstanding which oddly didn't feel like a misunderstanding but more like a horrible—horrible case of *déjà vu*.

'I was talking about the Tremount and Carla,' she murmured very slowly. 'I rang her while you were out. Sh-she told me you...'

Her voice trailed away. Her eyes went blank. Her father—the Bressingham, she found herself repeating. Goose-bumps began to break out all over her wet skin. Then, no, Carla and the Tremount, she corrected herself.

'Y-you bought it,' she continued with a perplexed frown. 'Carla s-suddenly thinks you're the bees-knees w-when only hours before she...'

She stopped again, frowning that perplexed look across the pool at André, who was standing taut and still and looking very pale. 'I n-need to sit down,' she said, and did so, stumbling over to the nearest pool chair and dropping into it.

Cold, she felt icy cold, and nothing seemed to be functioning. Heart, lungs, the blood in her veins—they'd gone very silent and still, as if they were gathering themselves ready for some kind of major eruption.

'Samantha…' That was André's voice, she recognised as if from a great distance. There were his footsteps she could hear echoing like thunder on the hard tiled floor. '*Cara mia*, listen to me…' And he sounded odd, rough and thick and…

'Why is there a door locked upstairs?' she asked him.

The footsteps stopped. She looked up, saw him standing stock-still about four feet away. 'It's a storeroom,' he said. 'I keep my personal files locked away in there…'

'Liar,' she said, and looked away again. He kept the door locked because it was Raoul's room.

Raoul—!

Oh, dear God! She jerked to her feet, jarring her knee in the process so she couldn't help but wince. André took a giant step towards her but she held him off with a trembling hand. 'No,' she said. 'I'm all right. I'm not going to black out. Just don't come near me for a minute while I…'

Once again the words dried up, flailing in a muddy pool of confusion she couldn't quite seem to clear.

'You're not all right,' he refuted hoarsely. 'You're beginning to—'

'Remember—' she finished for him. And just like that it finally happened, roaring up with the abruptness of a flickering flame sizzling in the short grasses of her memory, suddenly erupting into a column of fire.

'Oh, my God.' She gasped, and began shake. André, her father, Raoul, the Bressingham. 'André,' she murmured painfully.

And he was there, coming from behind to drop her robe about her shoulders then holding it there with hands like vices that began firmly pulling her back from the edge of the pool as if he was afraid she was going to topple right back into it.

Maybe she *was* about to topple. She didn't even care. The flame of truth was a roaring column inside her head. It began leaping, flicking out long lethal fingers across huge empty gaps to ignite other memories.

'You lied to me,' she whispered.

'By omission, yes.' His deep voice confirmed.

'You deliberately set out to cheat and deceive me.'

His hands tightened fractionally. 'I wasn't like that,' he denied. 'You were given only half the picture. The rest was—'

Without trying to listen she broke free, somewhere in the recess of her burning mind surprised that he actually allowed her to do it. She limped off towards the door that opened into the beautiful sitting room. Behind her, André followed in grim silence as she crossed the room to the walnut bureau, tried to open it and found it locked.

'You took the key with you when you left here,' he quietly informed her.

Key, she thought, and bent to feel around under the bureau's base, then came back up with a fine-worked gold key stuck to the middle of a piece of sticky tape. It was a spare key, originally taped there by her mother and allowed to remain in its secret place when the beautiful piece of furniture came to Samantha. She had been fifteen years old at the time, and inconsolable with grief. But to touch the smooth walnut wood had been like making contact with her mother. She did the same thing now, gently stroking the wood and immediately feeling that special sensation.

Then tears flooded into her eyes, because she suddenly realised she didn't have a single thing like this to remind her of her father. Not any more anyway. André had taken it all away from her.

Holding back the tears, she concentrated on fitting the key into the pretty ornate lock and easing back the roll-top lid. It slid into its housing with a smooth familiarity that clutched at her heart.

Inside the bureau were more memories. Precious, special, deeply personal memories slotted neatly into a row of finely worked cubby-holes. Letters, birthday cards, photographs...it was a diary of memorabilia spanning her whole life.

Then there were the other things. Things which didn't belong in here. But she'd thrown them in and had locked them away just so they were out of her sight.

The flame burned brighter. She had no control over it. It showed her the Bressingham, her father, Raoul, then the Bressingham again, planting faces, buildings, snatched little scenes into her head like picture postcards, before burning each one of them up in a sheet of fire to replace it with another. She saw herself on her wedding day, dressed in white and smiling. Dressed in black at her father's funeral and inconsolably sad. A hotel foyer virtually reduced to a pile of rubble. André scowling. Raoul smirking. Typed words written on pieces of paper she couldn't quite focus on well enough to read.

'You betrayed me,' she whispered.

'No, I didn't,' André denied.

'Where's Raoul?' she asked next.

'In Australia.' He seemed prepared to answer her questions as they came. 'He's been there for the last twelve months.'

There was a significant reason why he'd offered up that last piece of information, but Samantha did not have the ability to work out what that reason was right now. She was too busy remembering other things: painful truths with wretched conclusions.

'He tried to rape me, right here in this house,' she murmured thickly. 'And you let him get away with it.'

No reply came back to answer that particular charge, she noticed. And she found she wasn't really surprised. When André had stopped himself from finishing his sentence this morning it had not been his stepfather he had been about to declare his love for—but his half-brother, Raoul.

Raoul, the younger one, the spoiled one, the mean and shrewd, manipulatively sly one... Though big brother was not above being manipulatively sly himself, she recalled.

The tears attempted to flood again. Lodging them back into her throat, she reached out and with trembling fingers picked up the set of angrily discarded papers. Not once had she looked at André since they'd faced each other across the swimming pool, and she didn't attempt to do so now as she turned to offer the papers to him.

'These belong to you,' she said. 'Raoul gave them to me.'

Lean brown fingers slowly took them from her. Her heart felt sluggish as she watched those fingers begin flicking through the copied pieces of evidence documenting the events leading up to André Visconte gaining full ownership of the Bressingham Hotel—on the same day that he'd married Samantha Bressingham.

'Quite a dowry, when you think about it.' She smiled on a tight piece of self-derision. 'The Bressingham came really quite cheap for you, didn't it?'

'Don't make judgements when you are not in possession of the full facts,' he grimly advised.

'You mean I still have some more ugly memories to look forward to? How nice.'

'Not all of them are ugly.'

'They are from where I'm standing,' she said, and walked away, out of the room and across the hall then up the stairs.

As she travelled along the upper landing she passed by the door to Raoul's room. Last time she had stepped through that door she had gone to confront him about those papers. Now she was glad the door was locked. She never wanted to cross its threshold ever again.

Shutting herself in the bedroom, she stood for a moment with her face covered by her hands. Her insides were trembling and her flesh was shivering, and her head was aching so badly she wanted to crawl beneath the duvet and go to sleep.

But that was exactly what she had been doing for the last twelve months, she told herself. She had been sleeping to hide away from the ugly truth that she had fallen in love with a man who had deceived and lied to her right from the start.

Their whirlwind courtship and hasty marriage had been a smooth, slick manoeuvre on his part to seal the deal of any hotelier's dreams of gaining possession of the Bressingham. And why had that been? she asked, slowly sliding her hands away from her face to stare bleakly at this next ugly truth.

Because the Bressingham was special. No one would ever try to dispute that. Old as it was, and tired as it was, it possessed a reputation for old-world grace and charm that had been capturing the hearts of anyone who walked into it for the last one hundred and fifty years.

Mention the Bressingham and people's eyes lit up, no matter where in the world it was that you mentioned it. It was that well known, that warmly thought of. That special.

It was why Stefan Reece's eyes had lit up when he'd mentioned the Bressingham. And it was also why he had directed his comments about the hotel directly to Samantha. Family-owned and run, from the day it had opened its doors to its first paying guests. And Samantha was now the last living member of that family.

But none of that silly, soft sentimentality gave the reason why people like André and Stefan Reece would do almost anything to own the Bressingham. No, for them its importance lay in two very simple elements.

Its premier location in a premier city and, quite simply, its name.

To buy the Bressingham name was to buy a dead-cert winner. So if push came to shove, and the daughter had to be bought along with the name, then, what the hell, why not? She was young, she was good-looking, she was great in bed.

'Oh, God, I hate myself.' Samantha groaned, and pushed her hands to her face again—only to drag them away almost immediately when a knock came at the door.

Nausea clawed at her stomach. 'Go to hell,' she said, and forced herself to move, walking on stiff legs into the bathroom.

She heard him try the door handle as she was shutting herself away, and wasn't surprised he'd ignored what she'd said. The man was immune to other people's feelings. Which was why she had locked the bedroom door so he couldn't come in. In that way, at least, she knew the man. He was no coward when it came to facing problems.

As opposed to herself, she likened sombrely. She had made a wretched vocation out of refusing to face hers!

Almost as if she'd just thrown down a challenge, her mind began to replay that ugly scene from twelve months ago. While she'd been shut away in this same room, taking a shower, Raoul had calmly walked into the bedroom she'd shared with André and had left the stack of documents on her bed, then gone to his own bedroom to await the outcome.

She'd known why he had done it. Only an hour before he had propositioned her, and she had slapped him down with the coldest little refusal she could use.

The papers had been his retaliation. So she'd read them, with a sickened disgust at how low Raoul had been prepared to go in his quest to cause trouble between her and André. Then she'd walked into Raoul's room to tell him what he could damned well do with his papers of lies.

But it hadn't turned out like that. Raoul had been clever; he had known exactly what he'd been doing when he'd lured her into his bedroom that night. Tall like André, dark like André, but younger, more like her own age, and with a mean streak a mile wide that he was oh, so careful never to show André.

'Oh, come on, Sam,' he murmured dryly. 'We all know you're a hot little thing. Even my macho brother never knows whose bed you're sleeping in when he's away.'

'That's a lie,' she said, going white at the poisonous suggestion. Then, 'Don't do that!' she snapped when his hands came up to touch her. She knocked them away and started backing up.

He smiled a lazy smile. 'But you're family,' he murmured tauntingly. 'And we all know how big brother likes us all to get our even share. It makes him feel good and in control. ''You want money, Raoul? Sure you can have money. You want a car? Sure, here's the cheque. You want to live in my house? Sure, live in my house; make yourself at home, what's mine is yours.'''

'Think again if you dare to believe he was including me in that,' she told him coldly.

'And why not you?' he jeered. 'Those deeds of ownership on the Bressingham tell you exactly where you stand in big brother's plan of things. You were a very un-hostile takeover, Samantha.' He spelled it out cruelly. 'Came with the fixtures and fittings. One feisty wife. Pain-in-the-neck flirt. Install her in family home. Use at will.'

'God, you're a nasty piece of work, Raoul.' She retaliated. 'I own the Bressingham!' she declared angrily. 'It came to me in my father's will!'

'Did it?' He sounded so sure of himself. So absolutely positive that he was right, it started her doubting her own mind right there and then. 'Did it actually say, ''I hereby bequeath my precious daughter the Bressingham Hotel and enough money to return it to the proud place it used to be''?'

He knew it didn't; she began to shake. Her father's will had merely stated that everything he possessed would go to her. André had taken care of the rest. And why not? She trusted him with her life, never mind her father's business affairs. She had been so grief stricken. So lost without the man who had been her mentor and her hero from the day she'd been born. She hadn't even known he was ill. He'd kept so much from her.

Had that included letting André buy the Bressingham?

Now she could see her own face as it must have looked that night in Raoul's bedroom. See the slow dawning of a realisation that Raoul could be right take the colour from her face. And if he'd been right about one thing, he could have been be right about the others. Maybe she had come with the deal. Maybe André had married her because her father had insisted that the Bressingham must remain with the Bressingham family.

Beginning to shiver again, she reached out to switch on the shower, then dropped her robe to the floor so she could begin peeling off her wet swimsuit. She didn't want to remember any more, but her mind decided otherwise. As she stepped beneath the shower's hot spray, the rest of the dreadful scene began to fill her head.

Raoul trying to touch her, her slapping his hands away, him enjoying the minor skirmish, smiling, taunting her with words and gestures until she could barely breathe as panic began stir. He was big, he was strong; she had been no match for him. What followed had been a horrible experience that had continued as a frantic struggle on Raoul's bed—when André had walked in on them.

And that is about as far as I want to go with this, she told herself on a sick little shudder. What she really needed to do was get to away from here—right away, she decided, on a sudden upsurge of panic that had her stepping quickly out of the shower. She needed to give herself some time and space to get her head together. Because, right now, she didn't know who she was, what she was, or even why she was!

* * *

André knew when he saw her coming down the stairs that he had a big problem on his hands. He had been standing here in the hall waiting for her, half expecting to see her wearing a cold mask instead of a face. But it was worse than that. She was dressed in stark, mourning black, and was carrying that damned suitcase she had brought with her from the Tremount.

Samantha was about to bury their marriage.

'Going somewhere?' he questioned silkily.

She didn't bother to reply. Neither did she make eye contact as she attempted to walk straight past him as if he wasn't there.

His hand snaked out, wrenching the suitcase from her. It brought her to a stop on a sharp little gasp. He was very happy to watch the anger flare in her blank green eyes. 'We need to talk,' he said.

'No,' she refused. 'I have nothing I want to say to you.' And she kept on walking—without the suitcase. Head up, body stiff, only that small limp to ruin her cold, stiff exit. It was almost a shame to spoil it, he acknowledged. But *he* was going to talk, he determined grimly. *She* was going to talk!

'Have you ever heard that old saying, if I had my time over, I would play that scene differently?' He fed the words coolly after her. 'Well, this is your chance, *cara*,' he said. 'Don't miss this rare opportunity you've been handed by playing the scene the same way again.'

Watching her pull to a stop, he felt the tight sting of triumph. She might hate the very thought of it, but she knew he was right. 'I can't talk about it all now,' she murmured unevenly. 'I need time to—'

'Time,' he grimly cut in, 'is something you've been wasting for twelve long, miserable months.'

'Okay!' She spun on him so abruptly that, even

though he had been deliberately provoking her into it, he didn't expect the speed with which she decided to take him on. 'You want to play the scene a different way?' she challenged. 'So let's play it a different way!'

And if he'd thought her cold a moment ago then she certainly wasn't now. She was burning with anger, with bitterness and a hatred that tried to sear off his skin.

'You walked in here that night, took one look at what was going on in that locked room upstairs, and instantly blamed me for it!'

'It was Raoul's room!' he threw back. 'His bed you were both tangled upon! Look at the evidence, Samantha. How would you have responded if that had been me with another woman in there?'

'Oh, no.' She shook her head. 'You are not going to divert the blame by shifting the argument. You were there. You saw. You drew your conclusion... I needed your help!' she cried. 'Instead I was called a whore!'

The truth cut deep; he went white. She was whiter. 'It was spur of the moment.' He defended himself. 'I lost my head.'

She wasn't impressed. 'Raoul said you never knew whose bed I was in when you weren't here,' she told him tightly. 'I didn't believe him. But it was the truth, wasn't it?'

'No.' He denied it, but he couldn't look her straight in the eye as he did so because, damn himself to hell, he had suspected she might *wonder* what it would be like to make love with other men.

The downside of marrying a virgin and finding himself landed with a feisty, flirtatious witch for a wife was that he just hadn't been able to trust her not to fly with her instincts and give those other guys a try.

'You didn't have to walk out of here the way you

did.' He heard himself grind out, and immediately acknowledged how weak that argument sounded.

Her eyes flicked green scorn at him. 'What else did you expect?' she asked. 'You threw Raoul out, then you returned to cut me into little pieces before slamming out yourself! I wasn't hanging around here to see which brother decided to return first and finish what he'd started. So I got out.' Her voice was shrill. 'What sane woman wouldn't?'

'I went to the Bressingham,' he explained. 'Spent the night in your father's old office getting drunk. Around dawn I had to finally admit that I had made a mess of the whole thing. So I came back here. You'd already packed and gone—so had Raoul.'

'At which you drew your own conclusions,' she inserted with a bitter little smile. 'No wonder it took you a year to stumble over me.'

'It wasn't like that.' He sighed. 'I—'

'I don't want to know.' Stiffly she turned back to the door.

'Devon,' he said, aware that he was clutching at straws now, to keep her here. 'Why did you choose to go to Devon?'

'Place of happy childhood memories,' she mocked without turning. 'We used to spend our holidays there. Staying at the Tremount Hotel, of all places,' she added with heavy irony. 'Which was probably why I felt so comfortable working there… Now you've bought it,' she said, and her voice began to thicken. 'Carla thinks you are wonderful and everyone is happy.'

'Except for you,' he responded gruffly.

'Yes.' She nodded. 'Except for me.'

'But why not?' he questioned frowningly. 'I thought you would understand that I bought it for you.'

She turned her head at that. 'Like you bought the Bressingham?' she posed, then smiled a wretchedly bleak smile and turned away again, and this time he could see she intended to leave.

Frustration licked through him. They had resolved absolutely nothing. She hated him. He had no defence. If she left now, it would be over. He was as certain of that as he had ever been about anything.

'Even a condemned man is allowed his moment to speak on his own behalf, *cara*...'

As he stood there, waiting to see what she would do, one of her hands fluttered up to touch her right temple. It was a gesture of uncertainty; already he had come to recognise it as such.

'I just can't stay here,' she whispered unsteadily.

'Fine,' he said immediately. 'Then we will go somewhere else.'

But the moment he began striding towards her she began to stiffen. 'I want to be on my own,' she murmured stubbornly.

'No.' The refusal was absolutely rock-solid. In any other situation he would have just taken hold of her and kissed her senseless, since he knew without a doubt that kissing was one sure way he could make her respond to him.

But that was just another scene they had played before, which now needed playing differently. So he sighed heavily and, ignoring her muttered protest, firmly turned her to face him.

'Have you any idea how frail you look?' he murmured gently. 'Give yourself a break, Samantha. Give me one!' he added. 'One split-second swoon and you could be under the wheels of the nearest car out there. So I am asking you, please, to let me come with you...'

He wasn't sure whether it was the *please* that did it, or the touch of his hands, or the way his eyes wanted to swallow her up whole. But something caused the wistful sigh of surrender.

'Come if you want.' She capitulated, then pulled out of his grasp.

Without hesitation he reached around her and opened the front door. Sunlight flooded into them. She stepped outside and paused to wait while he pulled the door shut behind them.

'Where shall we go?' he asked as he came to stand beside her.

'The—the Bressingham,' she responded unevenly. 'I n-need to see what you've done to it...'

CHAPTER TWELVE

From the moment she stepped through its heavy oak and glass doors, Samantha felt the tears threatening to fall once again. Beside her, André stood silent and still, waiting for her first response.

'It's finished,' she whispered.

'With the greatest test yet to come.' He smiled briefly, following her as she walked forward until she was standing in the middle of the foyer where she began to turn in a slow circle, taking in every dearly loved, perfectly reproduced detail as she did so.

'Nothing's changed.' She breathed out eventually, in a fantastical voice that drew another mocking smile. 'Okay.' She allowed. 'So everything has changed. But…'

She was truly overwhelmed by what she was seeing. In fact she found she couldn't quite believe it. The last time she had been standing right here the whole place had been reduced to a building site. She had not long since buried her father, and it had felt like the end of a special era.

Now everything was back right where it should be. The same look, the same smell, the same aged patina on the same pieces of oak, felled centuries ago and since preserved by layers of lovingly applied beeswax, many of which she had applied herself. Even the same lazy old staircase ambled up to the mezzanine dining hall, she saw, whereas the last time she'd been here there had been only a great ugly hole.

Drawn towards it by a power stronger than will, she walked up a few steps with fingers trailing the rich dark wood banister as if she was making contact with a long-lost friend; then she turned to take in the scene from this new position.

Born in the hotel, she had lived here and worked here from the time she had been old enough to carry a plate without dropping it. Her soul resided here in this great old building. Her birth name hung above its doors. She knew every quaint nook and cranny, every piece of wood, every vase and ornament or gold-framed painting on the walls.

And everything, everything was back where it should be.

'So...what do you think?' André prompted.

It was like asking a new mother what she thought of her baby. 'It's...perfect,' she whispered.

Oh, she wasn't so lost to sentimentality to ignore the fact that there were, in truth, many changes. Having felt the weight of the two-inch-thick health and safety report, she was well aware that, behind this outer dressing, the hotel had been virtually gutted and rebuilt. But what had risen from the rubble turned her heart over.

'I can't believe it,' she said, referring to what the architects and designers had managed to achieve.

'Why?' André's deeply dry voice queried. 'Did you expect me to put the *Visconte* stamp on it the moment your back was turned?'

If nothing else, his remark made her focus on him for the first time since they'd arrived here. He was still standing where she had left him, a lean, languid figure wearing an impeccably cut suit and a cynical smile.

Her own expression changed, cooled and hardened fractionally. 'I would rather do this by myself if you're bent on spoiling it for me,' she said coolly, watching his cynical look change to a grimace in acknowledgment of her chilly set-down, and she looked away from him again.

'Who took over the project after I—left?' she asked after a moment.

He began walking towards her. 'The whole thing came to a halt for a while,' he confessed. 'Then the contractors starting yelling at me to let them get on with it, so...' He shrugged, paused to look around him. 'The final result is pretty impressive,' he opined. 'I'm pleased that you are pleased with it.'

'Is the rest of it as impressive?'

He declined the invitation to give an opinion. 'I'll let you be the judge of that.'

'You didn't answer my question,' she said as he drew level with her.

'Which one was that?' he posed.

'About who took over the project after I left it.'

'Only one other person was qualified to do so,' he drawled with a self-mocking smile which sent her eyes wide in surprise.

'You mean—*you* took it over?'

'Don't sound so shocked.' He scolded. 'Being the very busy, hotshot tycoon does not absolve me of the right to a few small pleasures in life.'

Her frown came back, along with a sigh in exasperation. 'Is it me or yourself you're mocking when you talk like that?'

'Both of us, I think,' he said, then added more neutrally, 'Come and take a look at what we've done with the famous Bressingham dining room.'

He placed a light hand to her lower back to urge her to turn. Her spine arched away from the heat in his fingers. Without comment he dropped the hand again, and together they walked up the rest of the stairs with her body still tingling from the briefest of touches.

Nothing had changed here either, she saw, drawing to a stop at the top of the staircase to simply absorb what was to her the loveliest room in the building. This was where life happened at the Bressingham, she recalled poignantly. A place where the hum of conversation blended with the chink of silver on china, and people relaxed in comfortable chairs while enjoying food prepared by gifted magicians. And it all took place beneath the great crystal chandeliers hanging from the ceiling, now beautifully restored to their original glory.

The old grand piano still stood in its corner. The same brick-dust-red paint still warmed the walls. All it needed was covers placed on the tables and she would almost believe she was standing here, by the same *maître d's* station, waiting to be seated for a romantic dinner.

With the man she loved…

The tears threatened again, pressing like weights against her throat in their desire to escape as a new set of memories suddenly rose up to haunt her.

'This is where we first met,' André murmured, telling her that his own memories were coinciding with hers. 'I'd come here for dinner and you were playing *maître d'*…

She'd glanced up from her table plan to find herself looking at the most gorgeous man she had ever set eyes upon. Samantha progressed the memory. Smooth and suave, breathtakingly sophisticated in a black silk dinner suit, he'd tossed a devastating grin at her, had touched a long finger to her black bow tie and had said, 'Snap…'

'You took my breath away.' André took back the moment. 'So much so that I think I said something really stupid, like "Snap" and touched your bow tie...'

Samantha swallowed. So did he.

'As I drew my finger away it brushed the underside of your chin, and it was like touching a small piece of heaven...'

'Don't,' she whispered unevenly.

'Why not?' he demanded. 'Don't you think the ruthless rat of a tycoon should be allowed any sentimentality?'

'I just don't want to talk about it,' she answered painfully.

'Well, I do—' And before she could do more than gasp out a protest, he placed his hands round her waist and, with the minimum of effort, picked her and plonked her back down again, right behind the old-fashioned *maître d'* station.

Her eyes leapt up to his and her mouth parted to issue a stinging rebuttal. But instead the words clogged in her throat and she found herself locked into a painful replay of one of the most precious moments in her life.

'That's right.' André growled. 'Look all wide-eyed and startled, just as you did that evening, and remember, *cara*, just who it is you're looking at!' His hand came up, a finger settling beneath her chin. The skin there seemed to actually preen itself. 'For I am the guy who took one look at you, with your glorious hair and sensational eyes, and skin like the smoothest substance I've ever known, and fell so head-over-heels in love with you that he would rather cut his own throat than *ever* hurt you!'

Angry—he was stunningly angry, she realised belatedly. All that cynicism and mockery had been hiding a deep and burning anger, which was now spitting out at her from eyes as cold as black diamonds in a face chiselled from the hardest rock.

'Then, why did you?' She hit right back at him, and if his eyes were hard hers were harder. With a toss of her head she dislodged the finger. 'I gave every single *cell* of myself to you—and you threw it all right back in my face! That isn't *love*, André! How dare you even call it that!'

'Are we talking about Raoul here, or the Bressingham?' he gritted.

'Both,' she said. *'Both!'*

A door opened somewhere below them. André turned like a serpent sensing attack as a woman in an overall walked across the foyer and disappeared through the door by reception.

'Who was that?' she questioned shakily.

'A cleaner,' he replied, swinging his eyes back to her with a new frustration burning in them, because the interruption had ruined the moment, and he knew he would never get it back. 'There is a whole army of them around somewhere,' he added, withdrawing his aggressive stance with a sigh. 'Where to now?' he asked coolly.

She shook her head, still shaking from their confrontation. 'I don't know,' she confessed. 'I—y-you choose...'

But André didn't want to choose. He wanted to grab her by the shoulders and shake some sense into her! 'Can't you see—can't you tell what I've tried to do here?' he bit out angrily.

'Kept to the letter of your contract with my father.' She nodded.

He sighed in frustration. 'Any second now,' he gritted,

'I am going to kiss that closed mind of yours right out into the open.'

'It is open,' she declared.

The glance he threw her actually made her skin flinch. 'No, it isn't,' he said, and threw her completely by walking away from her.

Watching him go, she felt a moment of sheer terror. No! she wanted to cry out. Don't walk away! Don't give up on me now, when I need you to justify your part in everything!

He stopped. She held her breath. Had she actually shouted those words out? Turning, he flicked her a lean look that told her nothing. 'Are you coming?'

Her heart clattered into action, relief swimming about her head while another part of her wanted to remain aloof and defiant. 'I—yes,' she said, and stepped away from the *maître d'* station. He turned his back and started walking again. She started to follow, acutely aware that, somehow, somewhere, control had shifted from her to André.

'Wh-where are we going?' Weakly she tried to grab it back again.

She hadn't got it, she realised as soon as he answered. 'Somewhere less...emotive to finish this conversation.' He supplied, as if throwing down a gauntlet.

But there was no such place inside this building. The moment they stepped into her father's old office, André realised his mistake, seeing the change come over her face. Maybe he shouldn't be doing this now, he pondered grimly as he watched the memories close around her. Maybe he should wait, give her the time and the space she wanted to recover properly, before they dug into the real issues clamouring around both of them.

Damn it, he cursed silently. How could she start to

recover without the full truth to help it to happen? Turning angrily away from his moment of uncertainty, he walked over to the place where anyone who had known the late Thomas Bressingham would also know he kept his private store of spirits. It was too early for whisky; André realised that. But right now he needed something.

'Has this room been touched at all?'

Her voice sounded thick with unshed tears. Grimacing, André added an extra tot to the glass. 'Other than being brought up to Health and Safety standards, no,' he replied, failing to add that it had been his strict instruction that nothing in this room must be touched unless it was absolutely necessary.

Strangely, though, he hadn't issued that instruction out of consideration for Samantha's feelings. He had done it for his own. He might possess a long string of premier-class hotels, but even to him the Bressingham was special... Just as Thomas Bressingham had been a special kind of man. This overcrowded, very male-orientated, private office held in its very walls some part of what had made his father-in-law special. He could never put his finger on exactly what that was, but he could always feel it when he stepped in here.

A little as his very tactile wife was feeling it now, he likened when he turned with his glass to find her wandering about the room, gently touching things with the caressing hand of a lifelong lover.

But then, she belonged in here too. A Bressingham. The last in a long line of Bressinghams.

'Let's talk about your father,' he said.

A light came on in her eyes then was instantly doused again. 'He loved this place.' She sighed out tragically.

Grimacing at the claim, André mentally took a deep

breath—and went for broke. 'But he loved you one hell of a lot more, *cara*...'

If he'd put a whip to her hide Samantha could not have been more offended. 'Because he was prepared to buy me the man I loved by giving this place to him?' she suggested painfully.

That was it. He might as well have said it. Samantha watched him put down his glass and close the gap between them with a swiftness that sent the breath deep into her lungs. Hands gripped her shoulders, heat speared through her body, catching fire...catching fire as it always did when he touched her. His eyes glittered down on her like black storms of biting fury and, with a small shake, he compelled her to listen and believe what he was about to say to her.

She wanted to refute it, even before she'd heard it; she knew she desperately; desperately needed to refute what was coming. When he opened his mouth to speak she almost, almost flattened her own against it just to stop him from speaking.

Then he began, his voice hard-edged with honesty. 'Your father did not give me this place to *buy* me, Samantha,' he told her very precisely. 'He gave it to me because he was broke.'

Full stop. No elaboration. His eyes said, Believe it. His silence said, Accept it.

'No.' she choked the denial of both.

'Yes,' he insisted, not angrily but so calmly that she knew it was the truth. 'He knew he was sick. He knew he was broke, and he knew that Health and Safety were threatening to close him down if he didn't spend millions bringing the hotel up to modern standards. So who better to pay the price than the very wealthy, very besotted future son-in-law?'

The cynicism was back. Shocked horror contracted her pupils until there was nothing left but dark green circles of truth. 'You think I set you up!' She gasped.

He released a hard laugh. 'I am not that short on self-esteem,' he returned then let go of her and turned to walk back to his drink.

But his hand was shaking as he lifted the glass to his lips. 'I don't believe you.' She charged him. 'It's the reason why you didn't trust me... Why you could believe Raoul's version of what happened that night instead of mine!'

'Let's stick to one problem before we starting dealing with another,' he clipped.

'If you drink one more sip of that whisky, André, you will have to suffer me driving you home!'

He rounded on her furiously. 'Who said we are leaving together?'

It shook her to the core. On a wave of hollowing weakness she stumbled into the nearest chair. The air throbbed, the anger roared like a lion in the sudden silence. He set down his glass; she pushed trembling fingers to her brow, where the muddle of memories were still struggling to sort themselves out.

'Ex-explain about the Bressingham, then,' she prompted eventually, taking his advice and trying, trying to stick to one problem at a time. But it was difficult, because they merged like two parts of the same whole and she couldn't seem to separate them.

On a harsh sigh, he sank down onto the edge of her father's desk, shoved his hands in his pockets, then sighed again.

'Your father knew he was ill. He needed money. So naturally he came to me.' His voice was no longer harsh, but just heavy. 'I offered to bail him out—no strings attached. But he was too damned proud to let me do that. So he came up with his idea of an acceptable alternative,' he explained, his tone alone telling her that it hadn't been as acceptable to him. 'He would give me the Bressingham on the promise that I would do what was necessary to keep it open. And I was to mention none of it to you,' he added wearily.

'But why?' she questioned.

'Why do you think?' He sighed. 'His precious daughter must be worried by nothing. Her wedding day was coming up. She had caught her prince. He wanted to—'

'If you don't stop tossing words like insults at me, I will probably pick up something heavy and throw it at you.' Samantha cut in.

'The old Samantha would have just gone ahead and done it.'

But the old Samantha died on a road in Devon, Samantha thought bleakly. And the new one was still struggling to evolve from what was left. 'Please, go on,' she invited stiltedly.

'There is very little left to say,' he murmured with a shrug. 'We came to an agreement where I would do as he asked. But because I had my own pride to consider here, I refused to take possession of the hotel until you and I were officially married—hence the date on the documents you were given,' he defined. 'It helped me to justify what I was doing.'

'Beginning our marriage with lies,' Samantha inserted.

'I'm sorry,' he said.

But it wasn't enough, because it was hard to forgive someone— No, she then amended that. It was hard to forgive the *two* people she'd loved most in the world for deceiving her the way they had.

'Was I so weak, so pathetic that you both felt you had to protect me from the ugly truth?' she asked painfully.

'It was the deal.' He looked away. 'I couldn't in all honour break it.'

'So instead you broke the vow to honour that you made with me,' she concluded. Then she remembered that André had actually suspected she was a party to her father's deal.

A silent conspiracy. She smiled bleakly at the idea. Even her father's will had been carefully worded, with a simple one-liner leaving everything *he'd possessed* to her. André had dealt with the details. She had never thought to question him. He probably saw that as further proof of her involvement.

Oh, what a tangled web, she mused emptily, and came to her feet. 'If that's it,' she said huskily, 'then I think I'd like to go now.'

'Go where?' he asked.

'Back to the house,' she told him. 'To pack.' Pack and leave the open way this time, the calm way. 'I don't think there is anything left to be said.'

'That's where you're wrong,' he countered gruffly. 'We haven't even touched the tip of the iceberg as far as explanations are concerned... And if you think I am going to stand by and watch you walk out on me again, Samantha, then think again.'

'You never watched the first time.'

'Raoul,' he breathed. 'It always comes back to Raoul.'

Raoul, yes, Raoul, Samantha agreed wearily. Who'd come to live with them in London only weeks after their wedding. Raoul who had played adoring half-brother while secretly resenting André for everything. His wealth, his power, his new English wife. Raoul, the poor relation, born to the wrong parent, he'd used to call himself—out of André's hearing, of course. He had wanted to be a Visconte but had had to make do with being a Delacroix.

'He's sorry, if it means anything to you.'

'Sorry?' Looking up, she sent him a huff of scorn.

'Deeply ashamed of himself.' He extended.

The fizz of anger began to rise again. If she could have stopped it she would have done, because she knew, by now, that she had taken more than she could safely manage to deal with.

'He abused my hand of friendship, my hospitality, my marriage and me,' she spelled it out coldly. 'I hope he will live with his shame for the rest of his life.'

'He will,' André confirmed.

'And you want me to pity him for that? Is that what your expression is saying?'

'Pity is better than bitterness, *cara*. And I should know,' he added heavily. 'Look what my bitterness did to us.'

So he was actually admitting that he *had* believed her to be a party to her father's overall plan? 'I think I hate you,' she breathed, turning away.

'Only think?'

'Go to hell, André,' she incised. And with that she walked, shaking, limping—hating herself for that limp because it ruined an otherwise precise exit.

Out on the mezzanine the chandeliers had been lit. As she walked down the stairs she could see the whole ambience of the foyer had begun to pull on its evening cloak. If the piano suddenly began playing behind her she knew she would be truly done for.

'He went to Australia,' a deep voice said quietly, stopping her as her foot made the foyer floor. 'I thought you'd gone with him, so I chased after the pair of you.

I went to kill him,' André admitted. 'Then I was going to strangle the lovely life out of you. Or at least,' he added, 'that was the plan.' Samantha sensed rather than saw the accompanying grimace. 'It didn't quite work out like that. I found him hiding out on a cattle station in God knows where because he knew I would be coming after him.' He released a short sigh. 'But it was really you I'd gone for. Except you weren't with him. So instead of killing him I broke down and wept like a baby... Does that help ease your pain to know that, *cara*?' he questioned levelly. 'It made a man out of Raoul, as twisted as that may seem. He broke down and wept right along with me. Then he told me the truth about what he'd done, and while I was trying to come to terms with the bloody mess I'd made of everything he disappeared again, leaving me alone to deal with the lousy, rotten truth of what the pair of us had done to you.'

Australia. At last she managed to recall where she had heard Australia mentioned before. Stefan Reece had seen André there twelve months ago. 'You were in Australia when I had my accident.'

'For two months.' His voice was coming closer. 'It took me that long to track Raoul down. And thirty seconds to realise what an unforgivable fool I had been. By the time I got back to London your trail had gone cold, and between wishing you in hell for leaving the way you did, and wishing you would just call me to let me know you were okay, I—lived—I think.' He sighed. 'I don't remember much about the long, empty months in between. Then Nathan Payne called me in New York with news about you, and my life suddenly kick-started again.'

'And Raoul?' she asked.

'Still in hiding in the outback, waiting for redemption to ease his guilt. I hear from him now and then, but nothing that says he has come to terms with the man he discovered himself to be.' His breath touched her nape and she quivered slightly.

'You've forgiven him.' She realised.

'After I had learned to forgive myself.'

'Don't touch me,' she said jerkily, hearing him move behind her. When he touched her she lost touch with her common sense.

'I'm not going to,' he replied—because he already knew what his touch did to her, and he was now trying to play fair. 'I just want you to consider forgiving Raoul some day, even if you cannot bring yourself to forgive me.'

And forgiveness was an essential part of her own healing process; that was what he was trying to say.

Funny that, she mused hollowly. But she had already forgiven André for some though not all of what he'd done—though she hadn't realised it until now. As for Raoul? She could now feel sorry for him, she discovered. But forgive? He'd scared her, seriously scared her, when he'd pushed her onto his bed. And it was the lies he'd told André about her, in an effort to save his own skin, she couldn't forgive. Those lies had helped to ruin her marriage—her trust in the one person left in the world she'd felt she could rely on—and had ruined her in a way.

'He gave me the copies of your deal with my father to hurt you too, you know,' she murmured.

'I know,' André confirmed, and didn't attempt to justify what Raoul had done.

A throb began to pound at the back of her eyes. A deep, pressure ache, which was trying to tell her she just couldn't think any more right now. On a slow, weary sigh her shoulders drooped, her body losing the will to want to her upright any more.

'You've had it,' André murmured huskily. 'Come on, let's get you home.'

Home, Samantha repeated silently, and didn't try to argue. She stepped forward; he followed, still maintaining his no-touch policy, she noticed.

The headache became so bad on the way back to the house that she could barely walk unaided up the stairs. Yet still André didn't attempt to help her. It was as if it had become a point of honour for him to make no physical contact without her permission.

But he remained right behind her all the way into the bedroom, and only left again when he'd watched her swallow two of her painkillers he'd produced from his pocket. After that, she pulled off her clothes and slipped beneath the duvet, frowning slightly because she had only just realised that the pills should have been in her bedside drawer; so how had he got hold of them?

She fell asleep thinking about the attractively innocuous puzzle.

CHAPTER THIRTEEN

ANDRÉ was sitting behind the desk in his study. Head back, eyes closed, bare feet propped on the desk top, and the soft light from a single table lamp just managing to diffuse the hardness from his weary profile. Since leaving Samantha to sleep away some of the strain of the day he had been working steadily, using it as his way of putting their problems aside, for a short while at least.

But now he'd had enough. Work could go to hell. It was his marriage that really mattered right now, and if he felt like wallowing in his own misery for a while then...why not? Across the room somewhere, Puccini's *La Bohème* was quietly filtering through the silence. His mood suited the music's dark mood, and one set of long brown fingers were idly rotating his black fountain pen to a rhythm he had unconsciously picked up.

But the fingers went still when he heard the first soft tread on the stairs.

His eyes slid open, but he didn't move. Lounging there, he stared at the gap in the half-open door, listened and waited to find out what she was going to do.

Go right past the door or step into the room? She had to see the light, hear the music. She must know he was in here. The new Samantha was as unpredictable as the old one, but he would lay heavy odds on the old one being unable to pass by that door without putting her head in here—no matter how reluctant she might be to do so. It was a point of pride—of defiance, if you like—

not to turn away from potential confrontation. She had done it only once in his experience, and that had been the time she'd left here one night a year ago, without hanging around long enough to have the whole ugly scene out with him.

Nothing happened. She hadn't moved towards the kitchen; she hadn't moved towards the front door. The muscles encasing his stomach began to tighten, trying to urge him to get up and go and check what she was doing out there. But he refused to give in to it. This was Samantha's move. He would wait here to see what that move was, even if it was killing him to do it.

The annoying, provoking, beautiful witch.

A sound at last. His heart stopped beating. His fingers curled around the pen. The door began to swing wider. Dressed to go or dressed to stay? he asked himself as a tingle that began at the back of his neck spread out to infuse his whole system with a state of readiness to move like lightning if she was dressed to leave.

Then she appeared in the opening, and he had to narrow his eyes to hide their expression as relief turned the tingle to liquid until his bones felt like wax.

She looked as she'd used to look in the mornings, all warm and soft and still a little sleepy. She was wearing one of her old short silk wraps in a soft shell-pink the same colour as her warm, bare toes, and her hair was lying in an unbrushed silken tangle about her face and shoulders.

'Hi,' she murmured awkwardly. 'I'm going to make myself some breakfast, if that's okay.'

'It's nine o'clock in the evening,' he said, frowning down at his watch.

'I know.' She offered a tense little lift of one shoulder. 'But I fancy porridge with honey… Do you want some?'

He shook his head. 'No, thanks,' he murmured, only to immediately wish he'd answered differently when she just nodded and disappeared again.

The first real invitation she'd offered him and he'd turned it down. What a bloody fool, he cursed himself. Now he had no real excuse to go after her. No excuse to get close, get *warm*—since he hadn't felt warm all day thanks to this wretched war of nerve ends they were waging on each other.

Closing his eyes, he relaxed back into the chair, cursed himself some more and managed to stay like that for all of five minutes, thinking of her wandering around the kitchen in that thin little wrap, and with nothing on her feet, and—

With a growl of frustration, he gave up trying to be strong, slid his feet to the floor, got up and went looking for her. She was standing by the microwave, watching a bowl of porridge rotate.

'Your father would disown you if he could see you making porridge that way,' he remarked lazily.

She looked up, smiled briefly, then looked away again. 'He *thought* he got his porridge the old-fashioned way every morning, but he didn't, the poor, deluded soul.'

'Found the honey?'

'Not yet.'

He went off to hunt it down in a cupboard, saw the kettle was coming to the boil with the teapot standing at the ready beside it. 'I'll have a cup of that, if you don't mind,' he said lightly.

'Sure,' she replied, and moved to pour boiling water onto the tea bags, took the pot to a ready-set table, before going back to get her porridge from the microwave.

Finding himself a cup, he sat down. She sat down. He

loosened the top on the honey pot then set it down in front of her. She picked it up and took the lid off completely, then picked up her spoon.

And because he couldn't help it, he started grinning. 'Finishing the day as we started it.' He explained the grin.

'One hell of a lot went on in between,' she dryly pointed out.

'How is the headache?' he queried belatedly.

'Gone,' she said. 'The sleep gave my head a chance to put its filing system in order, I think.' Twisting a spoonful of honey out of the jar, she then let it spiral its way down onto her porridge.

His mouth began to water. He didn't know why, but the warmth suddenly heating certain parts of his body told him that his mouth *wasn't* watering because he fancied the look of the honey!

It was the woman and what she was doing that was making him feel—

'You were right about something you said today,' she murmured.

'Only one thing? I must be slipping.' He grimaced. 'What was it?' he asked, lifting his eyes, up to her eyes to find them watching him from underneath her long dark gold-tipped lashes.

She licked the honey spoon. It could have been deliberate—but probably wasn't. Whatever, he felt his body stir, his own eyes darken in response.

'Bitterness hurts almost as much as the reason for it,' she said. Then she licked the darned spoon again with the full flat surface of her pink tongue.

'So you've decided to do what?' he prompted from somewhere way at the back of his overactive hormones.

'Try to put it to one side, I suppose.' She shrugged.

She dipped the spoon into the porridge now, and began eating it.

In dire need of something casual to do, André picked up the teapot and began pouring. Then he thought, To hell with it, and threw caution to the wind.

'You know, I've been thinking too,' he said, pushing a cup towards her. 'Has it occurred to you that if you hadn't had your accident and lost your memory you probably would have come back here eventually?'

'I know it.' She surprised him by admitting it. Then surprised him again with an impish smile. 'Got the memory back,' she reminded him. 'It's telling me all sorts of things I'd forgotten about.'

Meaning what? He wanted to ask, but didn't dare in case he didn't like the answer. So he stuck doggedly to the point he had been trying to make. 'Well, don't you think that if you had come back we would have gone through more or less what we have been doing for the last few days? Only, you would have been angry instead of frightened and bewildered,' he added. 'And I would have been digging my own grave by maintaining my lofty position as victim, because pride would not have allowed me to accept I was in the wrong when it would have meant my grovelling at your beautiful feet.'

'Would you have done—eventually?' She looked really curious to know.

'Haven't I been doing that in one way or another?' he countered ruefully.

'When?' Putting down the porridge spoon, she replaced it with the teaspoon from her saucer. 'When have you actually got down at my feet and grovelled for forgiveness for anything?' she demanded, calmly using the teaspoon now to dip into the honey pot again.

His loins began to tighten in anticipation of another

round of sensual torment. The porridge was gone, which meant there was only one place that spoonful of honey was meant to go. His eyes suddenly felt as hot as the rest of him.

'Put that spoon in your mouth and I will give you a full demonstration of how a man grovels.' He growled at her.

The spoon became suspended halfway between honey pot and her parted mouth. The air began to sizzle. His body was infused with that tight tingle of readiness to move like lightning if she forced him to. All it needed was for that spoon to finish its journey and there was no way, now, he could back away from a challenge he had thrown down without thinking it through first.

Spoon in mouth, I go for her. Spoon laid down, I stew in my own damned frustration.

Her eyes began to glow. His began to burn. The spoon went into her mouth. He was around that table before she had a chance to do more than drop the spoon and shriek, 'André, no!'

'André, no—you little liar,' he gritted, lifted her to her feet and kissed her hotly.

She melted as the honey had melted into the hot porridge. Slow and smooth, sensual and sweet. She couldn't even hold herself upright. His arms tightened around her; his mouth lifted free. He tasted of honey, she tasted of honey, the air swirled with its seductive scent.

'You've been gunning for this reaction since you came down the stairs,' he accused, his voice like gravel.

'That isn't true!' she protested.

'No? Then, why the skimpy robe?' He challenged. 'Why are you wearing nothing beneath?' Her cheeks grew hot. He grinned like a tiger with his prey all neatly tied up and ready to eat. 'You knew I was sitting down here worrying about you. You knew I'd be waiting like some slavish lap-dog for you to give me permission to leap. So I've leapt,' he gritted. 'Now let's see if you like what the lap-dog turns into when he's aroused.'

'You are no lap-dog!' She flashed the words at him scathingly. 'More a scavenging wolf, feeding on the remains of those weaker than you!'

'Are we talking about the Bressingham and your father again?' He sighed out wearily.

'And the Tremount. And the lies!' Her eyes flashed all hell and damnation at him. 'And the arrogant belief that you only have to touch me to make me bend to your will!'

'The lies, I apologise for. The Tremount, I don't,' he said. 'And the last little truth is your own cross to bear, *cara mia*, not mine!'

And to prove it, he kissed her again. She bent, she melted, she groaned and cursed him and kissed him back as though her very life depended on it. He picked her up in his arms and started walking, mouth to mouth, giving her no chance to come back down to earth again.

Out of the kitchen, down the hall and past the study, still bathed in soft light and the sound of Puccini. Half sobbing in his arms, she was so annoyed with herself for letting him do this. He walked the stairs with his lungs beginning to burst—not from the work of carrying her, but because he needed her so badly he was barely managing to control himself.

The bed awaited, still with the cool white duvet thrown back and the imprint of her body pressed into the sheet. Laying her down on that same imprint, he finally broke the kiss so he could straighten and begin taking off his clothes.

The little witch just lay there and watched him, bold

as brass. 'If you want this to stop, say so now,' he gritted on a sudden twinge of conscience.

'What's the use?' she said. 'When we both know you only have to kiss me to change my mind again?'

Had there been resentment in that voice? No, he decided, not resentment, but resignation to her lot, and the eyes were dark and languid, luscious and green and sensually wanting.

'Take the robe off, then,' he instructed.

She didn't even bother to object to his autocratic tone! She simply did it, wriggling herself out of the silk and casually tossing it aside so she could go back to what she had been doing—which was watching him undress.

Her eyes fluttered down as he began releasing his trousers—and remained there watching with the sensual blatancy of a woman who knew what was to come.

He was very aroused and, like her, he was quite blatant about it. As he stepped up to the bed, she reached out a hand and stroked him. That stroke said, Hello, you're mine. And the passionate way he responded said, Yes, I know.

Even as he eased himself down beside her she was welcoming him, arms up, eyes dark, hair a shimmering splash of fire on snow-white percale. 'I think you set me up for this, downstairs,' he murmured suspiciously.

'Mmm,' she said. 'What did you expect? A grand announcement that I'd given up the fight and decided to forgive you?'

'Why the sudden change?' he asked, gently tracing the delicate oval of her face.

'I just woke up and I wasn't angry with you any more,' she explained. 'So I decided to seduce you. It always worked in the past, when we'd had a row.'

'This was no ordinary row, though, was it?' he pointed out.

'No.' Her eyes clouded for a moment. 'But I also woke up remembering how much I love you.' She sighed out soulfully. 'I'm victim to my own emotions. It's really very tragic, when you think about it.'

'You little liar,' he gritted. 'You woke remembering how much *I* love *you*. Don't think I don't remember that smug look in your eyes over the honey spoon.'

His hands reached out to draw her so close that their mouths were almost touching and their eyes had nowhere else to look but straight into each others.

'I loved you more than any man deserved to be loved,' she whispered sadly, 'and you threw it all right back in my face.'

'I know.' And he did know. It was a truth of his own he'd had to bear the weight of for twelve long, miserable months.

'But I fell so fast and deep for you that it knocked me for six,' he confessed. 'There you were, a completely new phenomenon to me. You were younger than I was used to, more impulsive, as unpredictable as hell…' His hand came up to touch a lock of silken fire. 'You flirted with any man who would let you; you teased the life out of me—I was both fascinated and infuriated by the easy way you had other men flocking around you.'

'I worked in a hotel,' she reminded him. 'It was my job to be friendly to people.'

'You were a flirt in your cradle,' André dryly responded. 'I have that on authority—from your father no less. It made me so filthy jealous to watch you behave like that with anyone else but me, that sometimes you were very fortunate I didn't turn caveman and drag you off by your beautiful hair!'

'None of that gives you the right to say what you did to me when you found me with Raoul,' she said painfully.

Releasing a sigh, André kissed her. It was an apology; neither of them saw the kiss as anything else. 'It wasn't only your head Raoul messed with,' he admitted heavily. 'I couldn't seem to move without him slipping in with some remark about the men he had seen you with. It was okay. I had no problem with his suggestive remarks when it was always my arms you slept in each night. But then your father died only a few months into our marriage. You were so inconsolable you wouldn't let me near. I resented that, *amore*. I resented you shutting me out yet seemingly being quite happy laughing and joking and smiling with other men.'

'They didn't expect to sleep with me,' she responded. 'And I could sleep with you but I couldn't—' She stopped to swallow the tears again.

'I know. I understand.' His hand moved on her hair again. 'You were having to cope with too many other emotions to have room left for what it was you thought I wanted from you.'

'It was always sex, André,' she whispered thickly. 'Every time I looked at you I saw desire burning in your eyes, and I...'

'You're wrong, you know,' he murmured. 'It wasn't the desire for sex, it was the desire to share your pain with you. And, as for the sex, I gave you what you only ever seemed to want from me—which made me feel like a damned good stallion but did absolutely nothing for *my* emotional needs. I only wanted you to love me.'

Unable to remain still any longer, she was so angry, she sat up and away from him, while André bent an arm beneath his head and watched her spark.

His other hand came up to rest on her back. It had been meant as a soothing gesture, but she turned on him like the unpredictable firecracker she was. Coming to lean right over him, she hissed into his face, 'I loved you! How dare you imply I didn't love you? I lost a year of my life because I believed I would never be allowed to love you again!'

His hand moved, caught her nape, long fingers tangling with her hair and, without giving her a chance to say another stinging word, he brought her mouth down onto his own—and quite simply shut her up.

His hands found her body and hers found his. He kissed her slow and he kissed her deep and she sank seductively into it. No more talk; it wasn't needed. This said it all for them, despite what they had been saying only minutes before. They couldn't argue with desire when love surrounded it. It was different, special. It was the true elixir of life.

So they made love like tender lovers, touching, tasting, slow and easy, hot and deep. Their senses knew each other. It was why Samantha had responded every time he'd come near; her mind could shut him out but her senses could not.

For André it was oh, so much more arousing to make love to her mind as well as her body. To look into her eyes and know she was seeing him—the man she'd married. The man she'd loved enough to do that.

So he made love to her in Italian. He made love to her in French—because she'd always loved him doing it and he wanted to give her back every single thing she had forgotten in the last empty year.

And she listened—hell, she listened with every single cell. As he slowly smoothly entered her he had never felt so energised in his whole life.

Afterwards he kissed her slowly back down to reality. He kissed her soft mouth, her closed eyes, the scar at her temple. When she opened her eyes they were heavy, liquid and loved.

'If I run away again, you'll come and find me, won't you?' she whispered, so very earnestly.

'Always,' he replied.

She sighed at that.

They slept in a close love-knot. When André eventually woke up, he glanced at the time and slid stealthily out of the bed, let himself out of the room and quietly went downstairs.

When he came back she was sitting up with the duvet trapped around her breasts. 'Don't tell me you've just bought another hotel in between orgies?' she said.

'No.' His smile was rueful because of her unwitting connection with what he had actually gone downstairs for. Coming to stand over her by the bed, he placed two packages down in front of her, then bent to murmur. 'Happy anniversary...'

It took her a moment to realise what he was talking about. Then her cheeks bloomed with colour, her eyes turned black. 'I forgot,' she said, and sounded as if she was going to start crying.

'Take it from me, I've got what I wanted.' He smiled. 'Here...open this one first, because it belongs to last year's anniversary...'

Fingers trembling, Samantha did as he said, tearing the plain pink paper away from the flat package folded neatly inside. Opening it up, she read the words on the piece of paper until the tears blurred them away. It was the deeds to the Bressingham. 'No.' She sobbed. 'You don't have to do this.'

'It was done a long, long time ago,' he quietly replied.

'About an hour after your father signed the Bressingham over to me, to be precise,' he added gently.

Her eyes flashed and, as unpredictable as ever, she turned on him like an angry cat. 'Why didn't you tell me this before, when I was spouting out all of that rubbish to you?' she cried. 'I feel an absolute fool now!'

'Good,' he said, and kissed her again. 'So you should, for doubting me.'

'And you didn't doubt me?'

'We aren't getting into this one again,' he ordained. 'It's our anniversary. So open your second package.'

Not sure she wanted to, Samantha did as he said. A sigh heaved from her. 'I don't believe this,' she said breathily, staring down at the deeds for the Tremount Hotel.

'I think these two might make you an official member of the tycoon club,' André drawled, then added lazily, 'Here, I think this is a good moment to put these back where they belong...'

These turned out to be a simple gold wedding band, which he slid onto her finger, following it with a glowing emerald circled by a ring of diamond fire.

Samantha sat staring down at the rings she'd left behind for so long that she wasn't really surprised when André prompted ruefully, 'Don't I even get a thank-you kiss?'

'I'm going to cry,' she told him with a shake of her lowered head.

'Will it make you feel any better if you do?' he questioned gently.

'No.' She shook her head again.

'Okay,' he murmured and reached out to push her down onto the bed then came over her to claim his own kiss.

When it was over, he remained poised above her, looking deep into her swimming eyes, with his own eyes very sombre. 'The Bressingham was always yours. I never considered it mine from the moment your father concocted his deal. But the Tremount is different,' he admitted deeply. 'The Tremount is to say thank you to it, for looking after you when I should have been doing it. And to say I'm sorry for ever doubting you.'

'Raoul is your brother and you loved him—just as I loved my father.' Reaching up, she placed a kiss to his sombre mouth. 'Neither of us expected either of them to deceive us, André.'

'Your father's deception was well meant. Raoul's lies were not. And I deceived you too, don't forget.'

'But I want to forget,' she insisted. 'With the freedom to choose, I want to forget it all now. Can we do that?'

Her green eyes pleaded. His began to burn. 'Sure,' he agreed. 'Anything you say while you look at me like that... And the honey was a killer, by the way.'

A diversion, Samantha recognised, and let him keep it.

'I saw it done on TV once,' she confessed with smile. 'I always meant to try it out on you but never seemed to get the chance before today.'

His sleek brows arched. 'Anything else you would like to try out?'

'Lots,' she breathed, her eyes darkening in line with the challenge. 'Anniversary present number one coming up,' she announced. 'I think you'll like this.'

And he did.

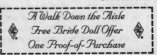

Together for the first time
in one Collector's Edition!

New York Times bestselling authors

Barbara Delinsky

Catherine Coulter

Linda Howard

Forever Yours

**A special trade-size volume containing three
complete novels that showcase the passion,
imagination and stunning power that these
talented authors are famous for.**

Coming to your favorite retail outlet in December 2001.

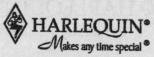

HARLEQUIN®
Makes any time special ®